A Beth-Hill Novel: Karen Montgomery Series, Book 1: Budget Cuts

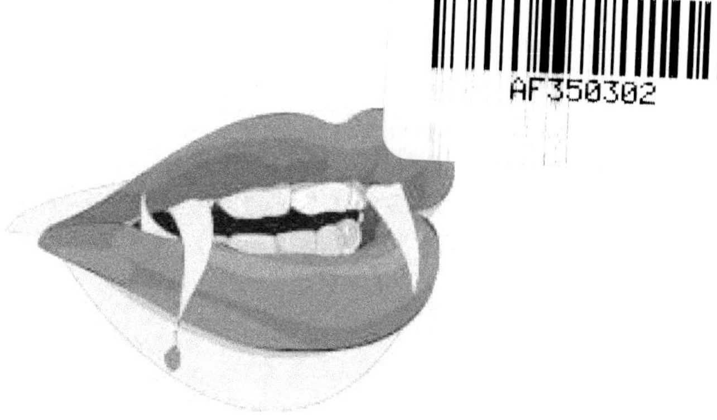

By Jennifer St. Clair

Writers Exchange E-Publishing

http://www.writers-exchange.com

A Beth-Hill Novella: Karen Montgomery Series, Book 1: Budget Cuts
Copyright 2007, 2015, 2023 Jennifer St. Clair
Writers Exchange E-Publishing
PO Box 372
ATHERTON QLD 4883

Cover Art by: Jatin and Sandy Cummins

Published by Writers Exchange E-Publishing
http://www.writers-exchange.com

The Book

"I wish it didn't have to be this way, but we need all the extra money we can get." We were halfway through a year fraught with monetary concerns, and the library was feeling the pinch. Eliminating Sunday hours had been the first step. The second step had been to cut the pages' hours until most of them had quit in frustration. The third step had been to close the libraries earlier, which had incensed both teachers and parents, not to mention the students who now had no place to study. The fourth step...layoffs. I parroted the director's next words in my head, lord knows I'd heard them enough. "If the library is going to survive this, we have to cut down to the bone."

My job was safe. Even a skeleton crew needed an Assistant Director/Building Manager/Technology Supervisor, but I would have given almost anything to remove some of the names from the director's list.

"You want me to fire every single one of these people?" I waved the list under the director's nose. "*All* of them?"

The director's lips pursed into a frown. "It's kinder to say layoffs, Karen. And I have faith you'll handle this with your usual tact." She picked up a folder and opened it; a clear indication that our interview was at an end.

Of course I would. I'd call the sacrifices into my office--separately--and leave a box of tissues in plain view on my desk. I'd school my features to show utter sympathy, and tell them that their career at the library was over until further notice. And I'd feel like the worst sort of hypocrite, knowing that my job was safe.

There were fifteen names on the list. Of the fifteen, I knew five employees by sight. Seven were pages, the rest of our small system's minimum wage workers. Two were relatively new hires, traditionally the first to go. And one, Ivy Bedinghaus, was listed as a Night Clerk at the Beth-Hill Branch Library.

"A what?" I stopped in the middle of the hallway.

Penny, the receptionist, gave me a startled look. "Ms. Montgomery?"

"Do we have any...Night Clerks at any of the other branches?" I asked, still staring at my list. Penny's name was not present. *Someone* had to answer the irate calls about why the library couldn't afford to purchase the newest John Grisham.

"Night Clerks?" Penny tapped a few keys and stared at her computer. "No, ma'am. Just the one. In *Beth-Hill.*"

She said the town's name as if I should have known some awful secret about it. I frowned at her. "What's so different about Beth-Hill?"

Penny hesitated, and a flush of red stained her cheeks. "Oh, ma'am, I don't like to gossip..."

Which was an outright lie. I'd caught her instant messaging her cousin in the next county over more than once. "Out with it. Why is there a Night Clerk in Beth-Hill and not anywhere else? What does a Night Clerk *do?*"

"Umm, clerk during the night?" was Penny's helpful suggestion. I glowered at her. "Oh, surely you've heard some of the *stories...*"

"Pretend I haven't." I kept a weather ear out for the click of the director's door, just in case, but I doubted she would emerge from her cave. *Give her a pot of coffee and an internet connection and she might not show her face until spring...* I forced my mind away from uncharitable thoughts.

Penny took a deep breath. "Oh, they're a bit...odd over there."

"Odd how?" Libraries were libraries, right? Granted, there were some *strange* librarians out there, but a whole town?

"Odd like..." Penny fluttered her hands through the air. "Like, there are *stories.*"

I sighed. "What kind of stories?" Penny mumbled something I didn't catch. "What?"

"*Witchcraft* stories. Beth-Hill was the site of a witch trial back in the 1800s. They've never recovered from that." Penny shrugged. "You weren't born here, ma'am. I don't expect you to understand."

I *didn't* understand, but I had lived in the area for ten years. The residents of small-town Ohio mistrusted anyone who couldn't prove that their ancestors had been founding fathers. And I had no way of knowing where mine had been when Beth-Hill had conducted its witch trial.

"What happened to the witch?"

"Oh, she wasn't convicted. If you ask me, she should have..." The phone rang, saving me from Penny's observations of the nameless witch's faults. I heard indignant sounds from the receiver, and abandoned her to her fate.

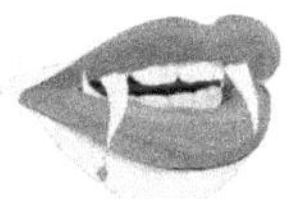

By Tuesday of the next week, I had whittled my list down to the last two pages and Ivy Bedinghaus. The box of tissues on my desk looked rather worn around the edges, and I had to bite my tongue to keep from sending unkind thoughts in the director's direction. This budget crunch was not her fault. And it *was* in my job description to maintain the daily workings of the library system.

By Thursday, repeated calls to the Beth-Hill Branch Library had netted me with nothing to report. Ivy Bedinghaus couldn't come to the phone right now. Ivy who? Oh, Ivy never arrived before sunset, and the evening reference librarian would know how to reach her. Employee records left me with an out-of-order phone number and an address that seemed to belong to a cemetery.

I was beginning to doubt that Ivy Bedinghaus existed. Perhaps some enterprising embezzler had created an employee out of thin air to cover their crime. According to her employee record, Ivy had been working for the library since 1954, when the Beth-Hill branch opened. She was well-past retirement age. I pictured a doddering old librarian, bent and wrinkled, carefully arranging the shelves every night in anticipation for the next day's crowd. It was a nice image, but it couldn't continue. Ivy Bedinghaus had to go. And since she wouldn't return my calls, I would have to find her myself.

I waited until dusk, hopped in my car, and drove to Beth-Hill, determined to set things straight. The branch, a tiny little building badly in need of repair, sat in the middle of a strip of storefronts. I saw two pizza places, a bookstore, a cafe, and what looked to be a coin shop vying for space with a movie theater (one screen), a bank branch, and a small general store. Very picturesque.

I pulled up in front of the library an hour before closing and walked inside to dead silence. The library clerk's eyes were closed, the reference librarian was nowhere to be seen, and a tiny wisp of a page pushed a loaded book cart to the back of the room.

There were no patrons in evidence. The daily newspapers sat neat and folded on the reading table, the new books--what little there were, at least--shone with fresh polish. The carpet, although old and worn, did not have a single speck of dirt on it, and even the book drop at the circulation desk looked brand new.

"Oh!" Plump, bespectacled Marla Peterson hurried out of the stacks. "Ms. Assistant Director, ma'am! I'm so sorry...Janet's allergies are acting up and she's been on medicine..."

The clerk snored. I thought about firing her on the spot, but her name had not been on my list and I had fired enough people this week. "Call me Karen. I'm here to speak to Ivy Bedinghaus. Is she working tonight?"

"Who?" Over the phone, I could excuse this strange forgetfulness, but in person, it was frightening to behold. Marla smiled and shook her head. "Are you sure you have the right branch, Ms. Assistant Director?"

"Call me Karen." I held out Ivy's employee folder. "And I'm *positive* I have the right branch."

"Oh." I watched her gaze for a spark of recognition as she read the scanty notes of Ivy's long career.

"She has to be close to retirement age, wouldn't you think?" I asked. "I'm sure you've heard about the cutbacks..."

"Oh, yes...of course. *Ivy.*" Marla tried to smile. "I've been working too many nights, I think. Ivy's a wonderful employee, Ms...Karen."

"I'm sure she is," I said gently, "but the library's budget has been slashed *again.* The other branches don't have Night Clerks..."

"I don't expect they do." Marla pursed her lips and stared down at the folder. "I don't expect they do."

"Can I see her?" I prompted. Overtime had been cut as well, and I'd been at work since seven. "I promise it won't take long."

Marla sighed. "If you must." She stayed silent until we reached the children's section. "Ms. Karen, I..."

But I had already spied the workroom door. I opened it and gave her my best professional smile. "I'll only be a minute." I stepped inside.

The room was dark, but a small light burned behind a set of metal shelving near the back of the room. I heard the unmistakable sound of books being put into order, and saw a shadow behind the shelves, hard at work.

"Ivy Bedinghaus?"

The sounds stopped.

"I'm Karen Montgomery, the assistant director. I've been trying to get hold of you..."

"Yes, I know." The voice wasn't old or feeble, but young and firm. I frowned and walked up to the edge of the shelving. The shadow didn't move.

"I'm sure you're aware that the library has experienced some terrible budget cuts."

Silence.

"We've done our best not to come to this point, but we have no choice. We're being forced to lay off some employees to save..."

When I stepped around the shelving, I saw the same young page I'd seen before. Her pale, wispy hair made her look even younger than she seemed at first glance. But when she met my gaze, I saw something *old* in her eyes, something I did not wish to examine fully. I stepped back.

"Where's Ivy Bedinghaus?" My voice sounded more frightened than firm.

The girl smiled. "I'm Ivy Bedinghaus."

"You can't be." I held out the employee folder. "Ivy Bedinghaus has been an employee of the library since..."

"February 13, 1954."

I narrowed my eyes. "You can't be more than sixteen."

Ivy tucked a strand of white-blond hair behind her ear. "Seventeen."

"If you're seventeen, then how can you..." I shook my head. "I don't know what kind of scam you're trying to run here, but..."

Ivy held up her hand. "Wait. I'll explain."

I folded my arms. "Please do."

"I've worked in this branch since it opened." For the first time, I saw something other than humor in Ivy's blue eyes. "I'm the one who rescued New Johnstown's books from the flood in '87. I've guarded the rare book room in the main library when Charlie needed a break. I've..."

"Wait a second. You've already said that you're only seventeen. Don't lie to me. And who's Charlie?" The only Charlie I knew of was the founder of the library itself, and he had been dead for fifteen years. And the flood had been before my time, but I *did* remember an odd story about it. Perhaps Penny would know.

Ivy bit her lip. "I'm sure he'll vouch for me."

"There isn't any vouching to be done," I said. "I have no choice but to let you go, Ivy. I hope you understand."

"But I'm the library's *oldest* employee!"

At the moment, I could have cared less if she was the library's *last* employee. "I'm sorry, Ivy. I have no choice. The library just doesn't have enough money."

"I'll work for half of what I make now," Ivy said, desperate.

"You only make minimum wage. Any less than that would be illegal." Although if she truly had worked since 1954, she should have been making a lot more than minimum wage. Yet another odd thing about her employee file. No raises. No reviews. I wondered what minimum wage had been in 1954. Two dollars an hour? Less?

Ivy's chin began to wobble. I glanced around for a box of tissues, but the battered desk was bare, save for the lamp.

"Do you *realize* how hard it is to find a job in this town?" Ivy wiped her eyes and turned away. The desk lamp threw her shadow against the wall and made it into a monstrous shape, dark and foreboding.

"The fast food restaurants are always hiring," I suggested. "And I'm sure they pay better than the library ever did."

"You don't understand," Ivy whispered.

"I wish I had better news, budget-wise," I said. "But it's only going to get worse. If this keeps up...I'm sorry."

Ivy's shoulders shook. And although I wanted to pat her back and tell her everything would be okay, that wasn't the professional thing to do. So I left her alone, and avoided Marla's accusing gaze as I walked back to my car and drove away.

That night, a howling storm swept into town and left three thousand inhabitants without power. The library's security system went haywire, and the security company called--you guessed it--me.

I grumbled something into the phone, pulled on a sweatshirt, jeans, and sneakers, and dashed through the pounding rain to my car.

The drive to the main library took over an hour. By the time I pulled into my designated parking spot, it was well-past the witching hour.

The emergency lights cast dim glows across the silent stacks. As I entered the foyer and disabled the alarm, I thought I saw a shadow slip past the nearest display of bestsellers, but the lights from a passing car dispelled any notion of an intruder. Still, it wouldn't hurt to check. The library needed good publicity for the next election cycle, if the levy were to succeed. After-hours intruders would not endear the library in the hearts of the public.

Empty libraries hold a certain mystique. The books loom in the darkness, both strange and surreal. In daylight, they're only books, nothing more. In darkness, they hold the keys to every impossible dream.

I ignored shifting shadows and half-imagined movement and tried to flip on the overhead lights. Nothing happened, of course. A faint thrill of unease crept up my back and made me shiver; I put that down to the chill in the air and began my rounds.

As I approached the Rare Book room, I thought I heard a whisper of sound. I stopped, straining to hear through the layers of insulating books, and heard the sound again. It was a voice, low and indistinct.

I stood and listened for a minute, trying to make out the words, but I couldn't hear clearly through the leaded glass doors that led to the Rare Book room. The leaded glass doors that *should* have been locked. I tried the handle. They weren't.

I glanced up at the portrait of Our Founder as I tiptoed into the room. He looked rather ghostly in the gloom, staring down at me from the top of his princely domain. If one of the librarians' had left a radio playing overnight, I'd feel like an idiot for creeping around in the dark, but it was my duty to investigate. I marked up another job position to my list. Assistant Director/Building Manager/Technology Guru/Security Guard. It was a shame that none of my jobs paid enough for me to spare the library its budget woes.

But when I saw who sat at the Reference Desk, I forgot all about feeling stupid. "You!"

Ivy Bedinghaus spun the chair around to face me. "I smelled you as soon as you walked in the door."

"You...you what?" I stared at her.

"I set off the alarm. I knew they would call you."

"But..." I valiantly tried to collect my thoughts. "No. I don't even want to hear it. Stay right there. I'm calling the police."

Ivy stood. "You're making a mistake, Ms. Montgomery."

I picked up the phone. "The only mistake I've made is..." My voice trailed away when I saw the elderly gentleman standing underneath Our Founder's portrait. "Who's that?" My mind didn't want to accept the resemblance between the man in the portrait and the slightly transparent man standing in front of the display case.

Ivy gently removed the handset from my grip. "Why don't you sit down, Ms. Montgomery? Charlie and I will explain everything."

"Charlie?" I croaked.

The man bowed. "At your service."

I think that was when I fainted.

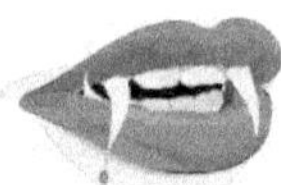

I awoke some time later to find I lay on the lounge in the staff break room. The comforting smell of coffee rumbled from the ancient percolator on the counter, and Ivy Bedinghaus stood in front of it, frowning.

I sat up and instantly wished I hadn't. The room swung around my head, and suddenly the smell of coffee wasn't so pleasant anymore. "What did you do to me?"

"You hit your head when you fainted," Ivy said without turning around. "I'm trying to make coffee, but..."

"Shake the pot a little. It sticks." That added yet another job to my list. Head Coffee Maker. Lord, yes. I leaned back against the wall and closed my eyes. Memory returned in slow trickles, aggravating what had to be a concussion. Perhaps I had hallucinated the transparent man standing in front of the display case. But I'd seen him *before* I fainted and hit my head.

And he had borne a marked resemblance to our late Founder.

"What's going on?" I demanded as Ivy poured me a cup of coffee. I had to sit up to accept it, but the room stayed put. "Do you realize I could have you arrested for breaking and entering?"

"I didn't break anything," Ivy said. "Charlie let me in." She sat down at the battered break table and clasped her hands together. "You have to listen to me, Ms. Montgomery."

"I can't do anything about your job," I said. "I wish I could. I wish..."

"Oh, but you *can*." I wondered if she knew how brightly her eyes glowed in the fluorescent lights.

"No, I can't." I set the untasted coffee on the table and stood. My legs wobbled a bit, but I thought they would hold me as far as my office. I needed to find a phone. "I'm sorry, Ivy, but I'm going to have to ask you to leave. If you're not out of the building in five minutes, I'm calling the police."

I must have been woozier than I thought. Ivy beat me to the door, and I didn't even see her move.

I gaped at her.

"Please, Ms. Montgomery." She had a stubborn set to her jaw now and a steely glint in her eyes. "Hear me out."

I stumbled back as she approached. "You can't..."

"One hour. That's all I ask." Ivy stayed in front of me, as if she expected me to rush to the door.

"This is...kidnapping," I squeaked, unnerved by the look in her eye.

Ivy shook her head. "No. If you decide not to help or believe me, then I'll let you go and never darken your door again."

"And if I decide otherwise?"

"Then you might be able to save the library and its budget and never have to worry about money again."

That was a nice thought, even if she *was* crazy. I sat down. "Okay. One hour."

For the first time that evening, Ivy looked a bit nervous. She took a deep breath. "First, you have to meet Charlie."

I followed her back to the Rare Book Room, clutching the cup of coffee like a life preserver. During library hours, of course, food and drink were forbidden in the public parts of the building, but I thought I might need something strengthening in my stomach, since I was about to formally meet a ghost.

A ghost. Just the thought made me wish I had stayed up to watch the Halloween special on the Discovery Channel last month instead of reading *Jane Eyre* for the fortieth time.

Ivy led the way into the Rare Book Room. I followed after a moment's hesitation. *One hour.*

"I have to admit that the afterlife isn't what I expected," a voice said near my ear. "Ms. Karen Montgomery. Assistant Director, Building Manager, Technology Supervisor, Jack-of-all-trades..." The voice sighed. "I remember those days fondly."

I came very close to dumping hot coffee down the front of my sweatshirt. "Damn it!"

Ivy giggled. "Charlie, that wasn't nice."

A wavery form appeared ten feet away, slowly coalescing into a dapper old man wearing a three-piece suit and carrying a straight black cane. He smiled at me. I gritted my teeth and hung onto consciousness with the rest of my strength.

"Charles Dalton, I presume?"

He bowed. "In the spirit. I'm very pleased to finally make your acquaintance. And I *do* apologize for frightening you earlier."

He frightened me now, but I wasn't about to admit that. "Apology accepted."

"Won't you sit down?"

My knees wanted to pretend they were made out of rubber, but I stood firm. "No thanks. I'd rather stand."

Charles Dalton favored me with a slightly incredulous look, then nodded and turned away. "As you wish. Are you at all familiar with the history of the library?"

I narrowed my eyes and tried to think. I remembered vague references, but my job had been to keep the library running, not to investigate things past. "I'm afraid not."

"My family used to be quite prominent in this town."

"Hence Dalton Street, Dalton Way, Dalton Park," I murmured under my breath.

Ivy glanced at me. I thought I saw a hint of amusement in her eyes.

Dalton continued as if he hadn't heard. "We helped build this town into what it is now, and some of us, a scant handful nowadays, decided to stick around to make sure Beth-Hill remained something to be proud of."

"If you were such prominent members of the community, why isn't the town named after you?" I asked.

"When Beth-Hill was founded, my great-great-great grandfather named the village Daltonsville." Dalton ran one shimmering finger down the spine of a battered book. "After his eighteen-year-old daughter was kidnapped by the fairies..."

"*What?*" But after that one shocked second, who was I to doubt his word? I was in the library talking to a ghost, after all. Why couldn't there be fairies? I waved my hand and sank down into a chair. "Never mind."

"Bethany Dalton was returned seven years after she vanished, but she never recovered," Dalton said. "My ancestor was so bereft by her disappearance that he changed the town's name three years before she returned."

I will admit to have wondered once or twice about the origin of the town's name. But I'd never asked anyone. If I had asked Penny, would she have told me the fairy story? Or would she have some mundane reason for the unusual name. Like Revenge, Ohio. I'd always wondered about Revenge, Ohio...

I wrenched my mind back to current events. "What does this have to do with saving the library?"

Dalton huffed into his moustache. "A little history never hurt a soul. And you need history if you want to understand what I'm going to tell you next."

I took a sip of lukewarm coffee and nodded for him to continue.

"After Bethany returned, my ancestor claimed the fairies owed him seven years of payment for taking his daughter from him." Dalton shook his head. "You can imagine what the fairies had to say about that."

I tried to smile. "I'm not sure I *believe* in fairies, but I'll suspend my disbelief for the time being."

Ivy sighed behind me. "Ms. Montgomery..."

"Ivy." The humor faded from Dalton's voice. "We discussed this."

"She has to know eventually." Ivy stood and crossed her arms. "I can't hide forever, Charlie."

"Don't tell me you're a fairy," I snapped. "This is a bit much. I can handle ghosts. I can even handle breaking and entering. But I can't..."

"I'm not a fairy." Ivy squirmed under my gaze. "I'm a vampire."

For the first time in my life, I couldn't think of a thing to say, except to repeat her words. "A vampire." I wanted to protest that she had to be delusional, but I was sitting in the Rare Book room talking to a ghost.

Ivy flushed. "Yeah."

I closed my eyes and counted to ten. When I opened them again, both Ivy and Dalton were staring at me with identical expressions of concern on their faces.

"And this is why, I presume, you're the *Night* Clerk?" My voice sounded a little strained. I struggled to remain calm.

"It really is difficult to find a job in this town," Ivy said softly. "I can't get a driver's license, and I..."

"Why can't you get a driver's license?"

Ivy's lips twisted in what might have been a smile. "The exam stations close before dusk. And they'd want my birth certificate, and social security card..."

That *could* pose a problem, especially if her appearance did not match the dates on her identification. No one would believe that Ivy was sixty-five years old. I had to remind myself that I didn't *really* believe her, but with Charles Dalton in the room, belief seemed to be a moot point. If ghosts could exist, why not vampires?

"So you're a vampire." I took a deep breath. "Okay. What does that have to do with your story, Mr. Dalton?"

"Do you know the tales about Fairy Gold?" Dalton clasped his hands in front of his waist and leaned on his cane.

"I know it never sticks around for long," I hazarded. Folklore had never been my forte.

Dalton nodded. "Fairies are tricky beings. They think it amusing just to put a glamour on garbage and leave it for unwary humans to find. The unlucky soul, thinking himself rich, might spend the gold to free himself from debt, then discover, days later, that his riches amount to a handful of rotting leaves."

"The...fairies did this to your ancestor?"

"They tried. But Jacob Dalton was too wily for even the fairies, and he insisted on a contract written in blood. But before he could act on the terms of that contract, he died."

That sounded a bit fishy to me. "Of natural causes?"

Dalton shrugged. The gesture seemed strange coming from a man of his stature. "No one ever proved he was murdered. Bethany was sent away to an asylum, where she eventually died."

"What about the contract? Did Jacob Dalton have other children?" I had to admit I was intrigued by the story.

"No, he didn't. I'm descended from his brother's son, and that side of the family was never interested in the supernatural. The contract was never found. And people searched for it diligently, mind you. That much gold, won square and fair from the fairies..." He shook his head. "Quite a few people got arrested for digging up the ancestral grounds."

"Which are..." There were quite a few old, rambling houses in Beth-Hill, but the village had no historical society to document its unusual history. "And what does this story have to do with saving the library?"

"The house sits right outside of town. You passed it on your way here, but you can't see it from the road." Dalton glanced at Ivy. "And the contract has never been found."

A glimmer of understanding took root in my brain. "Wait a second." I stood. "You don't seriously expect me to believe..."

"If you found the contract and forced the fairies to pay up, the library wouldn't have to want for money, Ms. Montgomery." Ivy was standing, too, her eyes radiating intensity. "And you're the only one who can find it."

I took a step back and banged into my chair. "Wait a second. Why am *I* the only one?"

Ivy was beside me, again without seeming to move. She put her hand on my arm. "Because Charlie and I know that you'll give the money to the library."

Unspoken words hung in the air, but I didn't want to listen to them. I licked my lips. "But the director wouldn't?"

"Giving the gold to the director would *not* be a good idea," Ivy said.

"Why not?"

Ivy and Dalton exchanged a glance I could not interpret. I sighed and let my question pass.

"Bethany had a child in the asylum," Dalton said softly. "For better or for worse, they let her keep her daughter until she was five, and then the little girl was farmed out to various uncaring relatives. She married a man by the name of Jacobs, and they had four children. Their second daughter, Amelia, married a man named Tobias Whitting, and they had two children. Amelia and Tobias divorced. When Amelia remarried three years later, her children took the name of their new father, James Huntington.

"Amelia's son died in a tragic accident when he was seventeen. The daughter, Karissa, dropped out of sight and resurfaced ten years later with three children and a hard-luck story her mother was happy to believe. Karissa's eldest daughter, Janet, married a man named Bernard Rubengia. They had..."

"I hope there's a point to this," I interrupted. "I've never been interested in genealogy."

"I'm almost finished," Dalton said, unruffled by my rudeness. "Bernard and Karissa had five children. Two died in infancy. One vanished, the black sheep of the family. The other two remembered their family folklore and wrote the stories down. Both died unmarried, spinsters to the end."

"I suppose we have the book in the library?"

Dalton glanced at Ivy again. "No. The only two copies in existence..."

"It took us a while to figure it out," Ivy said, picking up the thread of the story. "Charlie knew right away, but I wasn't so sure, until he showed me an ancient photograph of Bethany Dalton."

"You found a photograph of Bethany Dalton?"

Ivy pulled a small photograph album from the bookcase behind the reference desk. She handled it with reverence and none of the hastiness of youth. When she'd found the right page, she passed the book to me.

I stared down at an oddly familiar face. The girl in the photograph was young, perhaps seventeen, which would place the photograph right before her abduction. She wore a white ruffled gown and a corset that cinched her waist so tightly my own waist ached in sympathy. Her hair looked to be light brown, and it was piled on top of her head in an artfully messy chignon. She held a book in one hand, a fitting testament to the Dalton's eventual founding of the library.

Her face looked *very* familiar.

I tried to say something, but my mouth wouldn't form the words.

"What was your mother's name, Ms. Montgomery?"

"Harriet." My voice wouldn't rise above a whisper. "Harriet Isington Montgomery. She...she died three years ago."

"Do you know anything about her family?" Ivy kept her voice low and soothing. "Her father, perhaps?"

I cleared my throat. "She was adopted. I never knew--or had the urge--to try to find her birth family."

Ivy handed me a purple folder. "You might want to look at this, then. It took us eight months to gather all the records."

Inside the folder was a copy of my mother's birth certificate. Her mother's name was listed as Annabelle Simpson. The father...Martin Rubengia, deceased.

"The black sheep of the family, I presume?" Both Ivy and Dalton nodded.

The next piece of paper was a newspaper clipping, detailing the tragic, fiery death of Martin Rubengia, who had perished while attempting to save his girlfriend from a burning building. Annabelle Simpson was in critical condition at the local hospital and eight months pregnant.

She had lived long enough to name her daughter Harriet. The orphaned baby was in the local papers for weeks after the incident, until a quiet couple by the name of Ann and Harold Isington adopted the infant and took her away from the hullabaloo.

"For a black sheep, he turned out to be a responsible young man," Dalton said. "That side of the family never amounted to much, in truth, but I'm proud to know he didn't..."

I tried to crack a smile. "Resort to a life of crime?"

"It's been known to happen."

"Did his parents know?" I wondered how they would have reacted. With surprise? Fear? Would they have insisted on adopting my mother?

"They were dead by then, and the spinster sisters moved out of state. No one connected the Rubengias with the Daltons, even though we were well aware of the connection farther back in the line. With no family to pay for his funeral, the townspeople took up a collection and gave him a proper burial beside Annabelle."

"I've been to their graves," Ivy said. "I can take you there, if you ever want to go."

"I thought you said you didn't have a driver's license," I said, more out of habit than any desire to know.

"I don't. But even vampires have friends."

Vampires. Oh, right. Were there more *in Beth-Hill, or was it a one-vampire town?* My knees gave out. I sank into a chair. I wanted to bury my head in my arms, but I set the folder on the table and faced Ivy and Dalton with only a small tremor of delayed shock.

"Okay. Let me see if I've got this straight." I closed my eyes and tried to force my thoughts into some semblance of order. "Point One: There's a contract somewhere that details an agreement with fairies for seven years of payment."

"Gold, if the stories are true," Dalton said.

"Do you know how *much* gold?"

"Jacob Dalton believed his daughter was worth her weight in gold," Ivy said. "I've read his diary."

"I suppose that's in the library as well?"

Ivy opened her mouth to answer me, caught a glance from Dalton, and subsided. "No."

I glowered at them both. "Point Two: I'm descended from Bethany Dalton. You've made that quite clear. What comes next? How am I supposed to find a contract that vanished over two centuries ago?"

"Ivy's been deciphering the diaries, but she hasn't found any clues."

"Could he have had the contract with him when he died?" I asked. "How did he die, anyway?"

"A wild horse trampled him to death," Dalton said. "It would have been quite simple for the fairies to use a Phouka or some other creature to kill him."

"And how do you know the fairies didn't take the contract and tear it up?" I had no idea what a Phouka was or did, and didn't really want to know.

"Jacob Dalton might have been unlucky, but he was no fool," Dalton said. "He hid the contract in a safe place."

"He mentions the contract in his diary, but he hasn't mentioned his hiding place," Ivy said. "I thought we could start at the house and work from there..."

"The house. Right. The ancestral home of the Dalton clan."

"It's been empty for twenty years," Dalton said. "But if he hid it anywhere..."

"It's a wild goose chase," I protested. "And I can't..." I looked down at Bethany's photograph. Seven years with the fairies. *Worth her weight in gold.* She had died in an asylum through no true fault of her own. And if we found the gold or the contract, and the money was given to the library...

I sighed. "Okay. I'll help you."

Ivy beamed. Even Dalton smiled.

I held up one finger. *"But.* We don't go charging willy-nilly into the breach. If we're dealing with..." I closed my eyes and felt a queer shivering in my stomach *"...Faerie,* then we need a plan of attack."

"Attack?" Dalton frowned and glanced at Ivy.

"Or, at least, a plan," I amended. "Instead of starting at the house, why don't we start at the source? Have either of you had dealings with Faerie before?"

"Not in this lifetime," Dalton said.

Ivy shook her head. "No. But I know someone who has."

This *someone* of Ivy's acquaintance lived in the middle of the State Park that surrounded Beth-Hill. I didn't dare ask Ivy if he was another vampire. My sanity had been shaken so many times already, I wasn't sure it could withstand another blow.

"He owes me," Ivy said. "I don't think he'll refuse to help us."

I rubbed my eyes. "This...friend of yours."

"Nathaniel," Ivy said. "And he's not really a friend. He just owes me a favor."

"Yes." I tried to find the right words to phrase my question, but my brain didn't want to deal with subtle niceties. I sighed. "Okay. Am I driving?"

We left Dalton behind in the rare book room. He tried to explain why he couldn't come with us, but I didn't understand half of what he said. It did make a certain amount of sense that a ghost would be tied to one place, and most of the folklore I'd read had dealt with that particular problem in vague references and snippets of tales.

At least the storm had stopped. I glanced up at the full moon just as a wisp of cloud covered it.

"This Nathaniel." I still couldn't quite put my question into words. "He's not..." I glanced at the moon again. "He's not a werewolf or anything, is he?"

Ivy snorted. "No. He's not a werewolf."

With only a couple of hours sleep under my belt, I had to use almost all of my strength to concentrate on staying awake. I turned down a gravel road at Ivy's instruction, and coasted to a stop when the road ended a mile later.

"What next?"

Ivy smiled. "We walk."

I eyed the dark forest in dismay. "Walk? In the middle of the night?"

"You can stay here," Ivy bit her lip. "It won't take me very long to reach their cave, and..."

"This...*Nathaniel* lives in a *cave*?" I closed my eyes and leaned my head against the steering wheel. "I'll stay here." My sense of adventure had packed its bags and left me hanging.

Ivy slipped out of the car. I tried to follow her path as she stepped into the forest, but she vanished too quickly for me to track. It didn't take me long to fall asleep.

An hour or so later, I awoke when someone knocked on the driver's side window. I almost expected to see a cop standing in the murky darkness, but it was Ivy, returned from her errand. A darker shape stood behind her, his face a white smudge in the moonlight.

Ivy tapped on the window again. I rolled it down.

"Nathaniel has agreed to take us into Faerie, but we have to leave now." She glanced over her shoulder at the dark figure of Nathaniel. "It will be dawn in three hours."

Urgh. That meant I'd been awake almost all night long. "Can I leave my car here?"

"No one will harm it." Nathaniel stepped closer and I saw him clearly for the first time. Dark hair swept down over his collar and outlined his face, which was too thin to be handsome and too...unearthly to be real. He wore normal clothes: jeans and a button down shirt that shimmered when he moved, but he did not seem comfortable in the confines of mundane clothing. Physically, he looked no more than nineteen, but when he met my gaze, I felt an odd sense of *oldness* from him, as if the weight of his gaze carried far more age than his physical form.

"Nathaniel, this is Ms. Montgomery, the Assistant Director of the library. Ms. Montgomery..."

"You might as well both call me Karen," I said, and opened the driver's side door. The interior light flashed on, blinding me for a moment until I closed the door again. I blinked to clear my vision.

Nathaniel smiled. "Karen, then. Has Ivy informed you of the rules?"

It was too dark, even in the moonlight, for me to see Ivy's flush, but she turned away.

"Rules?"

"You cannot eat or drink in Faerie, even if you feel that you are starving. Never stray from the path, and try your best not to insult anyone." He spoke with a stilted formality, choosing his words with care.

Fear tried to close my throat. What had I gotten myself into? "Okay." My voice emerged as a squeak.

"Ivy, you should have told her this." Nathaniel's voice was mild, but it carried an undercurrent of anger even *I* couldn't miss.

"I thought it would be more plausible coming from you," Ivy whispered.

Nathaniel's mouth twisted. "I see." He turned to me. "Are you ready?"

"As ready as I'll ever be." I stared into the dark forest and fought back a shiver. "How will we get to Faerie?"

"I'll lead you there." Nathaniel pressed a small flashlight into my hand. "Use it if you must, but use it sparingly."

"Thanks," I said, surprised. His hand was cool and dry. "So." How did one find the correct phrasing for such a personal question? Should I even ask him? I took the plunge. "What are you? A fairy? A werewolf? Another vampire?"

He glanced at me. I thought I saw a touch of amusement in his eyes. "Actually, I'm a member of the Wild Hunt."

The Wild Hunt? I struggled against the insane urge to laugh. Nathaniel's face blurred in my sight.

"Ms. Montgomery?" Ivy sounded worried.

Nathaniel touched my arm. I pulled away, one hand locked over my mouth as I fought against disbelief. A tear slid across my fingers, sparkling in the moonlight. I couldn't seem to catch my breath.

I slid down the side of my car and hugged my knees to my chest.

"Ms. Montgomery?"

Nathaniel crouched in front of me, his face a careful mask of neutrality. "Will you survive this?"

The odd question shocked me out of my misery. "What?" My voice cracked. I tried again. "What do you mean?"

"Is it so much to realize that what you thought you knew as fact was wrong?" His voice was as gentle as a summer breeze. "That there is more to life than modern man can ever imagine?"

I considered his question very carefully. "No. I suppose not."

Nathaniel smiled. "Then don't fight it. Accept it."

I snorted. "That's easy for you to say. You're a..." *member of the Wild Hunt, dammit.*

He waited, silent. Ivy hovered behind him, her face lost in shadow.

I took a deep breath. "If you're a member of the Wild Hunt, how can you be human, too?"

Nathaniel grinned. I told myself it was my imagination that made his teeth seem sharper than they truly were. "I would not be able to help you if I were merely a Hound."

I straightened up. My knees tried to buckle, but I locked them into place. "What else?" I directed my question to Ivy, who retreated from my tone of voice.

"What else?" She laughed, nervous. "I'm not sure you want to know. Even now..." She bit her lip and looked away.

Nathaniel's sudden frown told me more than I wished to know about his relationship with Ivy Bedinghaus. He did not trust her, and I wondered why.

"Ivy." His voice raised the hair on the back of my neck. "You asked me to help you contact Amalea's family. You did not tell me why." All at once, I saw the Hound in him, the same sudden stillness as a dog about to lunge. I almost expected him to growl.

She shrugged. "You wouldn't have agreed to help us if you knew the whole story. But now that I have your word..."

Indecision struggled in Nathaniel's gaze, along with the knowledge that he had been outmaneuvered. He bared his teeth and closed his eyes. I *saw* him hold back the beast.

"Very well." His voice did not betray his fury. "You have my word. I will take you to Faerie, but that is *all* I will do."

I expected Ivy to explain to him of our quest, but she shrugged her shoulders again and nodded. I stared at her, appalled by her rudeness.

"Ivy, what will it hurt to tell him?" I put on my Assistant Director persona and folded my arms. Vampires, ghosts, hounds...Assistant Directors had to be prepared to deal with almost everything, but they had not covered the supernatural in library school. But I was well aware that my inexperience in dealing with the supernatural put me at a marked disadvantage. Ivy had set up this meeting; and it was up to Ivy to explain her reluctance to tell Nathaniel of our Quest.

Ivy frowned. "I'm sorry. I didn't think you'd need to know."

"If you intend Amalea harm..." Nathaniel left the threat unsaid, but he didn't have to voice it.

"At the moment, all we want to do is ask a couple of questions," I said before Ivy could speak. "It concerns a bargain Faerie made with an ancestor of mine and whether or not it was ever fulfilled."

"It wasn't," Ivy snapped. "I would have found proof if it had been."

"Faerie is a place, not a person," Nathaniel gazed at me for a moment, then transferred his gaze to Ivy. "What type of...bargain was this?" His eyes narrowed. "And why the secrecy?"

"You owe me a favor, and I have your word," Ivy reminded him, her voice cold.

Nathaniel stiffened. For a moment, I thought he might lash out against her, but he held himself stiffly in place, his eyes narrowed to slits.

I touched his arm. His muscles jerked under my fingertips. "I see no reason not to tell him, Ivy."

Ivy's bad mood vanished as quickly as it had come. She rubbed her eyes and shook her head. "It involves gold."

Nathaniel raised an eyebrow. "I think I've heard this story."

"Not many people have heard it," Ivy said. "It's died out, in modern times. I think the last time someone printed the legend in a newspaper was more than thirty years ago."

"You forget. I've been here for much longer than thirty years." Nathaniel glanced at me. "The *elves* made this bargain. Faerie is only where they live."

He looked no more than twenty. I opened my mouth to ask, then remembered Ivy had been working at the Beth-Hill library since 1954, and she was only seventeen.

"I think we're wasting time," I said, breaking the silence. "The longer we stand here arguing about it..."

Nathaniel shook his head. "I wish you luck, but prying gold from the elves is like..." he glanced at me, "trying to pry a book from a librarian's cold dead fingers."

"Very funny," I said sourly.

He did not smile. "That was no joke."

And on that pleasant image, we made our way into the forest.

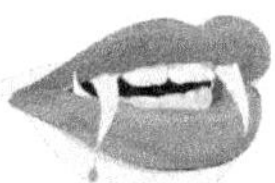

I like nature. I really do. I hike on occasion, and have been known to go camping once or twice. But walking through a forest in broad daylight does not hold a candle to walking through a forest in the middle of the night.

We walked in silence for the most part, with an occasional outburst from me or Ivy, who seemed to be just as ill-suited to hiking at night. Nathaniel, on the other hand, slipped through the grasping trees like water, a pale smudge of shadow in the darkness.

After what seemed like hours but was, in fact, fifty-five minutes according to my watch, Nathaniel stopped in front of an overgrown cave.

He turned to me. "I must have your word that you will not disclose the location of our home to anyone."

I laughed. "You're assuming that I could find my way back here?"

A fleeting smile touched his pale lips. "I must insist on having your word, even then."

"You have my word."

"Thank you." His eyes were silver in the moonlight. "Wait out here for a moment." He vanished into the cave.

I rubbed my arms and tried to wash the stain of sleepiness from my mind. My jeans were soaked, my shoes squished as I stamped my feet and tried not to imagine lying in a warm bed beneath toasty sheets.

"He shouldn't be long." Ivy glanced up at the sky. "He has to get permission to bring us..."

A white Hound slipped out of the cave, glowing in the darkness. It regarded us for a long moment, then sneezed and melted back into shadow.

Goosebumps made the hairs on my arms rise to attention. I tried to speak, but my voice vanished under the choking hold of fear. "What was that?" I gasped.

Ivy smiled. "*Who* was that would be the proper question."

"Okay, then who was that?"

"One of the Hounds."

I could see where the fearful legends of the Wild Hunt had started, if all the Hounds looked like that one. And their leader...

A tall, white-haired man stepped out of the cave, bending low so his head could clear the opening. Nathaniel appeared behind him, diminished in the company of his Master.

The Master of the Wild Hunt had white hair, true, but he was more ageless than aged. His face was smooth and unlined, his eyes cold. He folded his arms and stared at me. I had no trouble meeting his gaze. His disdainful expression reminded me of some of the library's more interesting patrons, the ones who expected to be served as if they were royalty.

I had the impression that the Master of the Wild Hunt was as close to royalty as I would ever get.

"You must be Gabriel," I said, dredging up the remnants of required reading for English Literature.

For a moment, surprise flickered in his pale eyes. He did not glance at Nathaniel, but I sensed some sort of communication between them.

"I'm a librarian," I said dryly. "It's my job to know these things."

"Do librarians know the perils of travel in Faerie?" Gabriel asked. His voice was low and perfectly without expression.

"Nathaniel was kind enough to enlighten me," I said.

Again, I sensed that silent communication between Hound and Master.

"So he did." Some of the coldness leeched out of Gabriel's bearing. "The elves will not welcome you."

"I don't expect to be welcomed," I said.

"And they will try their best to thwart you from your path."

"I imagine they will."

Gabriel stared at me. "I'm not sure you realize..."

"I have to deal with patrons who don't want to pay their fines, patrons who lose the library's books and try their best to not have to pay for them, and patrons who think it's a good idea to cross out all the words they don't agree with in the dictionary. I think I can handle elves."

Ivy stared at me.

I folded my arms. "I'm not the Assistant Director for nothing, you know."

"Evidently not." Gabriel still did not look convinced, but he seemed disinclined to argue further. "Very well. Nathaniel will accompany you on your journey." His gaze settled on Ivy for the first time. "And I trust he will owe you nothing after this?"

Ivy stiffened. "I did him a favor. And he said..."

"I know." Gabriel's voice hardened. "But my Hunt does not make it a habit to owe favors to anyone."

For a moment, Ivy looked like she wanted to argue, but she bit her lip, glanced at me, and subsided. "After this, yes. He will owe me nothing."

"I will put my own charge on my own Hound," Gabriel said softly. "Nathaniel will lead you into Faerie. And he will make sure you return...whole."

Not for the first time, I realized I had stepped sideways into absolute strangeness. I had no basis for normality anymore, and going to work Monday morning--if we got out of Faerie alive--seemed too mundane to be real. The supernatural world was the only true truth in my life for the moment. I could think of nothing else.

I took a deep breath. "You don't need to make Nathaniel responsible for our safety."

"No, I don't," Gabriel said, "But I have." He turned and ducked back into the cave. "Follow me."

Compared to the darkness of the forest, the cave was rather well-lighted and free from damp. Coarse sand crunched under our feet as we followed Gabriel to the back of the cave where a wooden door had been set into the rough-cut wall. The door would have looked at home at the front of someone's house, but it was totally out of place in a cave. I thought I saw something shimmer across the scuffed wood when Gabriel turned the knob, but it could have been a trick of the wavering light.

"Welcome to my home," Gabriel said.

The door opened into a narrow corridor lined with flickering torches and embroidered tapestries along the wall. At the end of the corridor was another door, this one a heavy oak monstrosity that would have looked at home in a castle. Gabriel's home, or what I saw of it as we hurried through, was built of gray stone. The floors were slate, the windows looked out onto a lovely garden, and the only color in the entire house stemmed from an odd assortment of knickknacks scattered around on dusty shelves.

A white Hound lay beside a faded couch, sound asleep. I saw twisted pink scars across his abdomen through his short fur, and wondered what had hurt him so badly. Another Hound lay with his head on the arm of the couch. He slept with a cute, white puppy who opened one eye at our approach.

I must have blinked, because in the space of an instant, the puppy had turned into a pale-haired baby who stuck her thumb into her mouth and closed her eyes.

I sensed the weight of Gabriel's gaze, judging my reaction of this new wrinkle in the tatters of my disbelief.

I swallowed hard. "She's adorable! How old is she?"

"Seven months old," Gabriel said. I detected the unmistakable aura of proud father in his bearing, despite his reluctance to show any emotion at all.

I kept my voice soft. "She looks like you."

Gabriel smiled. This time, his smile reached his eyes. "Thank you."

We passed the sleeping trio and walked out into the garden. Pale orange roses in full-bloom held court over a garden that would have looked at home in the English countryside, save for the trees that surrounded it.

I turned to glance back at the house. It looked like something out of a dream; rambling and mysterious, even in the half-light of dawn.

Dawn. I glanced at Ivy, but she seemed unconcerned. I frowned. Were the legends wrong about vampires and sunlight? Or had this whole night been an elaborate prank?

"Sunlight in Faerie harms no one," Ivy said, correctly interpreting my frown for what it was. "No one knows why, but we have a certain amount of protection here."

"And that is why vampires aren't allowed in Faerie," Gabriel said mildly. "The Hunt's standing with the elves is shaky enough. I shouldn't have to warn you to tread carefully around them."

I didn't need any warning, not after watching his daughter shift so smoothly from Hound to human. I wondered if Nathaniel could do the same thing. How could I face mundane work knowing what I knew? I closed my eyes and gathered my courage. Whatever happened between now and Monday morning, I couldn't stop now. I couldn't turn back. If I could persuade the faeries--the elves--to honor their bargain with Jacob Dalton, the library wouldn't struggle for funds ever again.

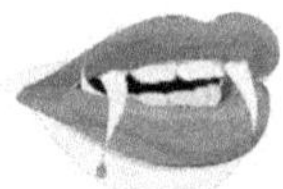

"There is a path," Gabriel said, and pointed into the trees, where I saw an arched stone gate. "I suggest you stay on the path and do not stray from it. Nathaniel will lead you to the elves and ensure they treat you well."

I hoped Nathaniel was up to the effort. In sunlight, he looked even paler than his Master. Was he still angry with Ivy for tricking him?

"Thank you."

The path was almost boring in its simplicity, but stunning in its design. Unless it had been made by magic, someone had spent endless hours forming a beautiful pattern from the shaped stones.

Nathaniel caught my arm. "It would be best not to center your attention on the stones. They tend to...shift."

Indeed, in the space of time that I glanced at him, the pattern changed into swirling spirals. I had no idea how the unknown artist had managed to fit the stones together so perfectly.

I tore my eyes away from the path. "Stay on the path; don't look at it?"

Nathaniel's lips twitched. "Exactly. If you must stare at something, stare at me."

That wouldn't be a problem, but he wasn't exactly my type. And for all I knew, Gabriel's Hounds had lives and lovers of their own. Was Nathaniel's sweetheart an elf, perhaps?

"So tell me about Faerie," I said, the librarian in me thirsting for knowledge. I bent to touch one of the pale bell-shaped flowers that grew along the path. It chimed. "How does one address an elf?"

"By name," Nathaniel said. "I'll be taking you to Lady Amalea."

"Amalea collects Shakespeare," Ivy said. "I found a copy of..." She swallowed the rest of her sentence and stared at the path. It had changed from spirals to a mundane row of bricks, save for clear crystal stones in what seemed to be an irregular pattern.

I had wondered what Nathaniel owed Ivy for. Now I knew.

"You stole a book from the library to give to..."

"No!" Ivy stared at me in horror. "It was a discard! I just..." Her voice dropped to a whisper.

I could not fault her for taking a book before it ended up in the library book sale or the dumpster behind Technical Services. I'd done it more than once, and I was sure the rest of the library's employees were just as guilty.

"Surely finding a book isn't as important as being charged to keep us out of trouble in Faerie," I protested. "Unless it was a *first edition* Shakespeare, and I *know* the library doesn't have any of those."

"It wasn't a first edition," Ivy mumbled, missing my sarcasm entirely. "It was..."

"It's hard to order books or get a library card when you have no identification and no address," Nathaniel said softly. "It's getting more difficult for us to function in modern-day life."

He wasn't only talking about the Hunt, I realized. What employer would hire a seventeen-year-old girl who didn't have a social security number or a valid driver's license? And how suspicious would they become when they realized their new employee, if, in fact, she *was* hired, hid from sunlight and never ate?

In this day and age, there would be other explanations, of course. People liked their privacy. No one wanted to pry. And yet, we were expected to give up that precious privacy for a taste of civilized life.

"And before you ask me why I didn't purchase the book at the library book sale," Nathaniel continued, his face grim, "you need money for that."

He didn't *look* like a pauper. His clothes, while not fashionable, were at the least functional, and seemed in good repair. I tried to imagine living without any income, but the prospect was too daunting for me to envision.

"Then how do you do it?" I asked. "How do you eat?"

"We are Hounds," Nathaniel said, as if that explained everything. In a way, I suppose it did. But that kind of life was as alien to me as human life was to them.

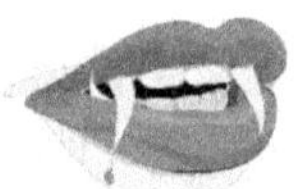

An hour later, the path branched. Nathaniel chose the fork without the cobblestones, the road less traveled, it seemed. Although clear of clinging underbrush, it held an air of neglect that made me distrust Nathaniel's intentions. Did I realize I had waltzed out into deep forest--in *Faerie*, no less-- with two supernatural beings I had just met? Had I lost my mind?

I stopped walking. The fear I'd held at bay awoke and clamored for attention. "Wait a minute."

Ivy glanced at me curiously. "What's wrong?"

"How do I know you're not planning to leave me trapped in Faerie?" I took a step backwards when Nathaniel turned to stare at me.

"I gave my Master my word that you would be returned unharmed."

Panic bubbled in my chest. "What do I know of Masters? Why am I here? I'm just...just a *librarian...*"

I had never felt such fear before in my life. It seemed to be a living thing, erupting from my chest like a demon borne from hell. I cast about for something familiar, something I could hold onto until the storm in my mind subsided, but I saw nothing.

"Damn." Nathaniel grabbed my arms before I could twist away. "It's the *spell.*"

"Spell? What spell? I don't feel anything..." Ivy's voice rose. "What spell, Nathaniel?"

Nathaniel ignored her in favor of me. "Karen."

I couldn't speak; couldn't protest that his grip would leave bruises on my flesh.

He shook me lightly. "Karen. It's a spell; nothing more. It's designed to keep humans away from the elves' territory."

"I don't feel anything," Ivy said again.

"You're not human," Nathaniel snapped.

His anger shocked me out of the circle of panic, but left me no less afraid. I twisted away from him, but he would not release me.

"Let me go!"

"The fear you feel isn't real, Karen. It's not coming from your heart. It's coming from the air you breathe; the ground you walk upon."

At the moment, I could have cared less. I kicked him, desperate to escape, and stepped off the narrow path.

The panic vanished. I faltered for a moment, strangely bereft.

"What *was* that?" My throat ached from screaming.

Nathaniel struggled to his feet, his face pale. He held himself stiffly, as if not trusting his legs to hold him.

I realized where I'd kicked him and felt my face flush. "I'm sorry. I didn't..."

He straightened with a groan. "It wasn't your fault. I forgot about the spell."

"A spell." I glanced at Ivy as I stepped back on the path, and tensed for the panic to return. Nothing happened.

Ivy breathed a sigh of relief. "Good. I felt the tail end of it, Ms. Montgomery. You..."

"Call me Karen," I said wearily. "Nathaniel, are you okay?"

He managed a smile that half-resembled a grimace. "I'll be fine."

"I'm sorry."

He waved away my apology. "It wasn't your fault."

My screams should have alerted the entire forest to our presence, so I wasn't very surprised when a horse stepped out of the forest a moment later. The man on its back--raven haired, pointy-eared, blue-eyed, and drop-dead gorgeous--held an unsheathed sword across his thighs, more a precaution than a threat, I thought.

I had the strangest urge to curtsy.

Nathaniel stepped in front of me. Ivy moved back, but not before she received a black glare from the elf on the horse. I had a feeling the elves liked vampires just as much as humans did.

"Hound." The elf's voice was far from courteous.

Nathaniel stood his ground. "Amalea will see us."

The elf sneered. "You seem so certain." And yet, he turned his horse and rode down the path without challenging any of us.

"You must be wary," Nathaniel said. "The Hunt has no...proper treaty with Faerie. I cannot predict how they will react after hearing your...demands."

"I'm not sure I'm in a position to demand anything, since we don't know if the contract still exists," I said. "At the moment...at the moment, I'm on a fact-finding mission, nothing more." Or, I thought I was, at least.

"You're not going to demand they deliver over several hundred pounds of gold?" Nathaniel asked.

"Where would I put several hundred pounds of gold?" I wondered what our Clerk Treasurer would have to say about that. Would the Director emerge from her cave for several hundred pounds of gold?

"How do you know it was *several* hundred pounds of gold?" Ivy asked curiously.

Nathaniel shrugged. "I've heard the story before."

He did not explain further. I wondered how much of the story he actually knew.

"How long has the Wild Hunt been in these parts?"

Nathaniel smiled, as if he suspected the turn of my thoughts. "Not quite that long."

We walked on.

Slowly, the forest began to change into gardens, airy and beautiful to behold. I recognized none of the flowers, but they were made even more beautiful by their alienness. We saw no more elves, but slim shadows slipped just off the edge of my sight, leading me to believe we were not alone. And, as we grew close to the edge of the sprawling gardens, we acquired an escort.

A small, cool hand slipped inside mine. I jerked away, then realized the hand belonged to a child with pale blonde hair and piercing blue eyes. She smiled at me and put her fingers to her lips. I tried my best to smile back.

Ivy and Nathaniel neither noticed I had stopped nor noticed I had acquired a child. I stared after them. My protests died on my lips.

The child tugged my hand and smiled again.

Both Gabriel and Nathaniel had warned me not to step from the path, but surely a *child* would do me no harm. I watched as Ivy and Nathaniel vanished behind a stand of bushes, and made up my mind.

I stepped off the path.

Sound returned as birdsong, faint and alien in the trees around me. The gardens had vanished, and forest now spread across everything I could see. Only the child remained a constant familiar presence at my side.

"Where are we going?" Each step we took darkened the sky above us, until full night reigned. Faint, luminescent fog hung in the air, wisps of glowing dampness that vanished as I passed through it.

The child tugged on my hand when I stopped to investigate softly glowing fungus at the base of a tree. We walked in silence broken only by my footfalls, and faintly, the sound of a flute.

A flute? Here?

As we approached, the music became louder and more melancholy. I heard a horse whinny to my right, but I could not see it through the trees. But when we stepped out into a small clearing, I saw the flautist and realized why I had been brought here.

A human girl sat on a large boulder in the middle of the clearing, her face aglow with moonlight and love. She wore a gown from an earlier era, and had pinned her dark hair up off her neck in a messy chignon. Even though she sat, I saw the rounded shape of her stomach and knew she was pregnant. The flautist, his honey-colored hair shining in the moonlight, lowered his instrument and took the girl's hand. "I've missed you."

"And I you," she responded, and threw herself into his arms.

The elf smoothed her hair and stared into the darkness of the forest that surrounded them. I stepped back, but the child pulled on my hand again, unconcerned.

I remembered the horse, and wondered to which lover it belonged. Was this after or before the bargain had been made?

"You shouldn't have come," the elf said, reluctantly pushing her away. "You know what will happen if they catch us together..."

The girl's face fell. "I had to see you," she whispered. "It's been..."

"Five months, fourteen days, seven hours, and twenty-one minutes," the elf replied. "Beth..."

I swallowed my gasp, even though I had already guessed their identities. The girl looked too much like me for it to be a coincidence. Somehow, I had traveled back through time. After the events of the evening so far, that didn't seem very hard to believe.

The scene abruptly changed. I stepped back as a room emerged from the forest, white and stark in the shadows around me. A woman lay in a narrow bed, her dark hair spread across the white pillows. She held two bundles in her arms.

"Two?" I heard myself whisper.

The child was not a child anymore; she had grown into a young woman as I stared at the twin bundles in Bethany Dalton's arms. Her honey colored hair flowed over her shoulders and down her back.

"Two?" I asked again.

The girl smiled and nodded.

When I looked back at the scene before me, it had changed again. The room stayed the same, but Bethany Dalton now stood in front of the barred window, alone. I could see by her reflection that she was crying.

A woman entered the room through a door I could not see, dressed in a starched, white dress. She wore a peaked cap on her gray hair, and she carried herself with obvious authority.

"Bethany, your daughter is asking for you."

Bethany Dalton did not turn from the window. "I have no daughter." Her voice wavered. "I have no daughter."

"You have a darling little girl," the nurse said patiently. By her expression, I assumed this was a familiar exchange. "She celebrated her fifth birthday yesterday."

"My daughter was stolen," Bethany whispered. "Stolen away..." She rocked an invisible baby. Her tears continued, unabated.

The nurse waited for a moment, to see if her words would have any lasting effect, but I had a feeling Bethany Dalton lived in a world of her own now, a world where she had *two* daughters, not one.

The scene changed again. This time, Bethany laid in her bed, asleep, her face turned towards the wall. Even in sleep, tears silvered her cheeks, as if she could not escape her sorrow.

A shadowy figure stepped into the room and spoke a soft word. A light flared up in the palm of his hand, casting enough reflection on his face for me to recognize him.

The elf from the forest stepped up to Bethany's bedside and gently took her hand. "Beth..."

More time had passed now; I saw gray in her raven hair, but her lover seemed unchanged. She turned her face towards his light, sunken eyes opening in wide surprise.

I saw scabs on her lips when she parted them to speak. "You."

"Time passes differently in Faerie; surely you remember that..." The elf closed his eyes, as if he, too, felt the pain of her bottomless sorrow. "I am sorry. In Faerie, I've only been gone a month, no more. And they would not let me return."

Bethany Dalton licked her lips. "A...month?"

"Perhaps two. Time passes quickly..."

"Yes. I remember." A faint smile appeared on her lips. "I remember."

"I came for our daughter, Beth. And you, if you'll come."

"Our...daughter?" Bethany Dalton frowned. "My daughter...my daughter was stolen..."

"You gave her to me freely, Beth." The elf stroked her hair. "Don't you remember?"

"My daughter is dead," Bethany said clearly. "Dead."

The elf dropped her hand. "Dead? But surely..."

"Dead. My daughter is dead." Bethany's eyes slid shut.

The elf stood by her side for a few minutes more, but she did not awaken. And I had a feeling that she had closed her eyes for the last time.

The scene faded, replaced by forest again. I saw the same rock, the same clearing, but Bethany Dalton did not sit bathed in moonlight.

The elf stood alone, his head bowed, his flute cradled in his arms. As I watched, he dug a shallow hole in the ground, dropped the carved flute inside, and covered it with earth, a fitting memorial to unrequited love.

The scene faded again. The child vanished from my side, but the boulder remained. At first, I hesitated to approach it, not wanting it to vanish and leave me without any landmarks at all, but I remembered the buried flute and thought I knew why the child had shown me the past.

It only took me a moment to dig it up. The instrument pulsed in my hands with a life of its own, fairly glowing in the sudden sunlight. I blinked to clear my sight, and heard someone call my name.

A moment later, Nathaniel burst from the forest, his eyes wild, as if he expected to find me dead.

"You vanished!" Ivy skidded to a stop beside him. "Ms. Montgomery, are you...What's that?" She stared at the flute in my hand.

"A flute." I stroked the carved wood and marveled that it had not disintegrated in its grave. "It belonged to the elf who was Bethany Dalton's lover."

Ivy opened her mouth, then closed it again, speechless. Even Nathaniel seemed at loss for words.

"And how did you manage to find it?" he finally asked.

"Bethany's other daughter showed it to me," I said. "I have my doubts that she's still alive, but..."

It felt rather refreshing to be on the shocking end of things for a change. I brushed past them and stepped into the woods. "Aren't we supposed to be meeting someone?"

Ivy and Nathaniel followed me in silence until we reached the path again.

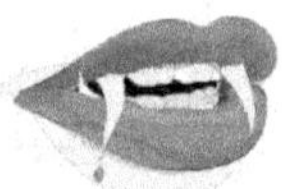

It only took five minutes more to reach the castle, and what a castle it was. If a castle could grow from a mountain, this would be the result. At times, I couldn't tell where the castle ended and rugged forest began. Only the evidence of windows, some cleverly disguised as caves, showed us the vastness of what had to be an ancient dwelling.

There was no moat; no portcullis, and as far as I could tell, no guards. But I had a feeling that the elves had no need of mundane guards, especially if they had more spells like the one that had caught me back on the path.

"They know we're here," Nathaniel said. "We only have to wait."

I chose a low-growing tree to perch on, and Ivy settled against an outcropping of stone. Nathaniel elected to pace, looking so much like a tiger in a cage that I wanted to drag him beside me and force him to relax.

Oddly enough, I had no fear of the elves. I thought I should be apprehensive, at the least, but I had found calm in some forgotten place and I was loath to release it.

Twenty minutes later, a girl stepped out of a hidden doorway and waited until Nathaniel noticed her presence. By his reaction, I deduced this was not his sweetheart, but he did not seem alarmed. He had a quick conversation with the girl I couldn't hear, then turned to face us.

"Follow me. I'm to take you to Amalea."

Ivy seemed subdued when we passed from sunlight into the dim interior of the castle. I didn't know why until I realized the absence of sunlight might be the worst drawback of vampirism. I wondered if the countless teenagers enamored of the vampire mythos realized just how hard it would be. And if vampires weren't usually allowed in Faerie...

Nathaniel led us through a maze of corridors, dimly lit with glowing chunks of quartz set into the walls. The striations inside the fist-thick crystals made them seem like living, breathing organisms instead of chunks of stone. Every once in a while, I thought I saw an insect or some other creature encased in the crystal, but I dared not investigate closely.

Nathaniel led us to a large room bare of furnishings. The walls glittered with chunks of colored crystals; a veritable treasure trove of precious stones. A tapestry hung along the far wall, depicting a serene forest scene that looked so real I mistook it for a window, at first.

A girl stood with her back to the tapestry, her gown moss green and richly woven. She wore a circlet in her flaxen hair, but no other jewelry. And when she smiled at Nathaniel, her entire face blossomed into something I would not hesitate to approach.

Ivy muttered something under her breath. Nathaniel gave her an unpleasant glance, then crossed the room to open his arms to his lady.

A moment later, he returned, with the Lady Amalea on his arm.

"Karen, Ivy, this is Amalea."

Up close, she looked even younger, but I felt a strange sort of power in her. Even this tiny wisp of a girl was a power to reckon with.

"I'm pleased to meet you," I said, and waffled over whether or not to hold out my hand. I finally did, and Amalea touched my fingers with hers, a small smile playing around her lips.

"Tell me why you've come," she suggested. "I won't offer you food or drink, so you needn't fear that."

It only took a moment to relate Bethany's tragic story, and a moment more for Amalea to realize what we intended to ask.

She sighed. "I truly wish I could help you, but you'll want to speak to my cousin, Kyren. He has more...history with that bargain than I do, I'm afraid." Her eyes fastened on the flute in my hands. "Where did you get that?"

I had a feeling both Nathaniel and Ivy wanted to know the answer to that question, since I'd given them a rather vague reply before.

I took a deep breath and told Amalea about the child, and the scenes in the forest.

Her face paled. "I thought you were the Assistant Director of the library!"

"I am."

"She's also the last descendant of Bethany Dalton," Ivy said smugly.

I watched as Amalea's face underwent a myriad of expressions. Last to come was understanding; she now knew why Ivy had recruited me.

"I see." She stared at me closely, shook her head, and sighed. "This changes things."

"In what way?" Nathaniel asked.

Amalea hesitated. "It's ancient history, Nathaniel. I'm not sure Kyren..."

"You're not sure Kyren what?" a new voice asked from behind us. I saw a strange emotion shimmer across Amalea's face before I turned around to face the newcomer.

The elf from the clearing had not changed at all. Or, rather, he had not physically changed; his hair was just as golden, his skin unlined. But his eyes...his eyes belied countless sorrows and a sarcastic smirk ruined the line of his mouth. He reminded me of the surly group of teenagers I had escorted from library property after they were caught smoking in the bathroom.

When he caught sight of me, the sneer froze on his face. Pain briefly flickered in his eyes, then died behind a mask of hauteur. "Who are you? Has my cousin expanded her entourage?" He glanced at Amalea, a mocking gleam in his eyes. "One Hound isn't enough for you, milady?"

I didn't see Amalea flush, but I heard her embarrassment in the tone of her voice. "I think you need to hear what they have to say. They came here for *you*, but they did not know it at the time."

"I do not consort with humans, and I most assuredly do not consort with vampires, Cousin." Kyren's gaze flicked to me again, and I saw the question there.

"We've come about Bethany, Kyren," I said, and raised the carved flute.

His reaction surprised me, but I don't think it surprised Amalea. Kyren staggered back, all masks gone in an instant. Raw pain seared his face into a rictus of its former self. And before anyone could offer comfort, or an explanation, he turned and ran from the room.

Silence reigned for a little while, as we stared after him in shock. Amalea was the first to move, shrugging off Nathaniel's arm to take my own.

"He did not mean for it to happen, you know," she said. "He...time in Faerie used to be different."

"You spend a week here and seven years have passed once you return," I murmured, and felt Amalea's surprise.

"Yes. For better or for worse, we've caught up with the Human Realm. Spend a day in Faerie now, and you'll only be gone for a day when you return. Eventually, the two worlds might pull apart again, but some of us like it this way." Amalea reached back to snag Nathaniel's hand.

I doubted she was the only elf to have a...different lover, but I imagined she was the only one who had fallen in love with a Hound.

"Is the other twin still alive?" I asked softly.

Amalea hesitated.

"Please. I don't care about the gold."

"But..." Ivy protested.

I silenced her with a glance. "Ivy, this is far beyond gold. This is beyond just saving the library. What I saw in the forest..." I remembered the light grasp of the child and shivered. "I've seen enough in the past few hours to make me believe almost everything. But..."

"It is the rare human who can accept Faerie and all it has to offer without batting an eyelash," Amalea said. "You're very brave."

I shook my head. "At the moment, I'm just numb. Just wait until I have a day or two to think about this. Mark my words..."

"You're doing fine," Ivy said, abandoning her protests for praise.

I honestly had my doubts, but I held my tongue and waited for Amalea to answer my question.

"No," she finally said. "Madeline died twelve years ago. Kyren was...devastated."

I did a rapid calculation in my head. "She was..."

"One hundred and seven," Amalea said. "Half-breeds have a longer lifespan, but not nearly long enough."

"How many...half-breeds are there?" I asked.

"More now than there were a century ago," Amalea said. "The rules and regulations have been relaxed. Nowadays, if Kyren fell in love with a human..." Amalea shrugged. "It would not be so surprising."

"But before? What happened then?"

"Bethany Dalton spent seven days in Faerie. When she returned to the Human Realm, seven years had passed. I heard, and this is hearsay mind you, that they had been meeting in secret for some time before she came here."

"And what happened?" I asked. "Why did she have to go back?"

"In those days, human captives were ransomed by their families or rescued by the Council. These days, there are no human captives; at least no legal ones. There are treaties in place, but occasionally someone makes a mistake or cannot resist a challenge."

"What happens to them?"

"If our Queen discovers their whereabouts, she lets them go. Or the Council comes to fetch them..."

She had mentioned this Council twice in the past two minutes. I hesitated, then decided I had to ask. "What is this Council you speak of?"

"The Council has nothing to do with the library," Ivy said. "Ms. Montgomery..."

"I think I'm entitled to know," I said mildly. "After all, I have a certain amount of Faerie blood. What is this Council?"

"A group of wizards and witches who attempt to keep the natural world and the supernatural world separate," Nathaniel said. "They enforce the treaties, police the area, and..."

"Stick their noses where they don't belong," Ivy muttered.

Nathaniel's lips twitched. "That too."

Ivy crossed her arms. "They wanted me to *quit*!"

I blinked. "What? Your job?"

"Yes. Ten or twelve years ago, they wanted me to quit." Ivy scowled. "I refused. And they warned me..."

"Warned you?" I echoed. For some reason, a vision of a Mafia hit man popped into my mind. "Warned you how?"

Ivy's voice deepened. "'We'll be watching you. If we discover any...anomalies here or anywhere else in the library system, we'll know who to blame.'"

"They don't sound very nice," I ventured.

Nathaniel glanced at Amalea, as if he expected her to speak. When she did not, he sighed. "There are only three Council members now. And they have other things on their minds. I doubt they would bother you now, Ivy. Who came to you? It wasn't Lucas, was it?"

"It doesn't matter," Ivy whispered. "I've already lost my job."

I flushed. "The library's finances have been cut so badly that we couldn't do anything else. We had no choice."

"Hence the gold," Nathaniel murmured. "It's beginning to make sense."

Amalea stared at me. "You were going to give the gold to the library?"

"I don't have much use for that much gold." I rubbed a chunk of dirt from Kyren's flute and wondered if he would return. "Should someone go talk to him, Amalea?"

"There's no need." Kyren's voice cracked. He appeared in the doorway Amalea must have walked through, its lines hidden in the intricacies of the tapestry. I realized that this castle was fraught with secret passageways and hidden doors. The elves seemed to love intrigue. "If you don't mind...I'd like to speak with..."

"Karen," I supplied.

"Karen alone."

Nathaniel stiffened.

Kyren waved away his concern. "I will not harm her. I promise you that."

Amalea took Nathaniel's hand. "We'll wait outside."

Ivy did not look pleased to be lumped in with Amalea and Nathaniel, but she followed them quietly.

Kyren did not move until the door had closed behind them. He waved his hand and an upholstered chair appeared in one corner of the room, faded, worn, and too comfortable for words. "Please. Sit down."

I sat, half-expecting the chair to vanish as soon as I sank into softness.

Another chair appeared across from mine, but Kyren did not sit down.

"That flute." His eyes told me nothing. "Where did you get it?"

"I think it was shown to me by a ghost," I said, realizing how ludicrous that sounded. But how could I explain away my presence in Faerie? It seemed I had to accept everything or nothing. There was no middle ground.

"What did you see?" Pain flickered briefly over his face.

I settled back in the chair and set the flute on my lap. The carved wood glowed beneath the coat of dirt. It only took a moment to tell him what I had seen. I didn't raise my gaze to his face until I had finished.

Kyren took a deep breath. "I see."

"Did you bring her back with you?"

Now he sat, and slumped in the chair as if his legs were broken. "Bethany? Yes. I did. But she only lived a handful of months before she died. She...she had been too long away from Faerie."

"And you never thought to search for the other twin?" I asked, struggling to remember her name. Had Charlie told me?

Kyren's mouth twisted. "No. Bethany insisted her daughter had died. I never doubted her word, even then."

How different would history have been if he had searched for the other child? "And the bargain you struck with Jacob Dalton?"

"I was worse than a fool." Kyren shook his head. "I wanted Beth back, you see, and that was the only way he would allow her to return."

"I heard he wanted the money to pay for his daughter's seven year absence," I said.

Kyren shrugged. "Tales grow in the telling, I suppose."

"But Jacob Dalton died before you could fulfill the terms of the bargain?"

"Jacob Dalton..." Kyren stared at the flute in my lap. "Jacob Dalton wasn't a very nice man."

Somehow, that didn't surprise me, but he had not answered my question. "Did you fulfill the terms of the bargain, Kyren?"

Kyren licked his lips. "You don't even know what the terms of the bargain were."

"Then tell me." I kept my voice soft.

"He wanted..." Kyren stood and paced back in forth in front of my chair, clenching and unclenching his fists. "He wanted gold."

"Yes. He felt Bethany was worth her weight in gold."

"No. Not just that." A sickly smile twisted his lips. "If that had been all of it...but no. He wanted the child. Or, children, as it turned out to be."

"He...wanted the children?" I didn't understand. *Couldn't* understand.

"Jacob Dalton's wife, Mary, died in childbirth when Bethany was two years old. According to what Beth told me, her father began to..." Kyren turned away, "...abuse her soon after. And the abuse didn't stop until she ran away...with me."

I knew, of course, that child abuse wasn't a product of modern times. But back then, abusive parents got away with a lot more than they would now. Sometimes, they even got away with murder.

"The story has changed over the years," Kyren said. "Such stories become more...romantic over time. The tellers twisted the events to their own designs, and everyone *knows* Faerie does not exist."

"Jacob Dalton was made the hero, and you were made the villain," I said, remembering Charlie's rendition of the tale.

"Yes."

"Did you seal the bargain?" I asked. "Did you..."

"To choose between the woman I loved and my own child?" Kyren's eyes flashed when he turned to face me. "Do you think me such a monster?"

"Then what did you do?" But even as I spoke, I realized his only course of action. "You killed him, didn't you?" I saw him flinch. "Or if you didn't kill him, you helped..." What had landed Bethany Dalton in an asylum?

"She had always been fragile," Kyren whispered. "And the strain of seeing her father's death was too much for her to bear. By the time..." He swallowed hard, "...by the time I found her, the babies were born. I meant to take them all, but I..."

"I imagine there are rules about murdering humans," I said softly.

Kyren sighed. "Yes. As it was, I brought Madeline with me and had to leave Beth and Sara behind. And when I returned..."

I remembered the bittersweet reunion, and Bethany's obvious distress. "When you returned, the woman you loved had lost her mind."

"The nurses and doctors thought she had murdered Madeline," Kyren whispered. "And I was too late, I thought, to save Sara, because Beth insisted she was dead." His mouth twisted. "And I was too steeped in grief to disbelieve."

"You had no way of knowing," I said. "That wasn't your fault."

He glanced at me, his eyes bright with tears. "Thank you. Your words don't help, but thank you."

"What happened to the gold?"

Kyren let out a long sigh. "I buried it. Hence the rumors of buried treasure, I imagine. Gold had a way of advertising its presence." He held up his hand to forestall my next question. "Don't even ask."

I held my tongue. "Thank you for telling me this."

Kyren nodded absently. "What would you do with the gold, if you had it?"

"I would give it to the library. We'd have enough money to hire back our staff and get through the next couple of years, at the least."

"You'd keep nothing for yourself?" He doubted me; I could tell by the tone of his voice.

"A coin, perhaps, to remind me that there *is* magic left in the world," I said.

"You wouldn't wish for fame? You've never wished for fortune?" He stared at me, confusion battling with helpless wonder.

"I've always wished I could live in a castle in Scotland, but what would I do once I got there?" I asked. "Collect books? I do that already. Buy new clothes? I like what I have. Not work?" I couldn't imagine quitting my job to twiddle my thumbs, even if my thumbs were dripping with diamonds. "I rather like my job," I said. "Except lately." Five years ago, I might have kept the gold, paid off my bills, and lived the rest of my life in bored luxury. But that was five years ago. I didn't have that many bills left.

Kyren shook his head. "Perhaps I have been too long from the Human Realm. I...expected less of you. I apologize."

I laughed. "You have nothing to apologize for. I don't blame you for doubting me."

Kyren took my hand, his face troubled. "I will think on this." He glanced up at the ceiling, as if he could see past the stone to the daylight beyond. "It's getting late. You should go back."

I left the flute nestled in the chair, and followed Nathaniel and Ivy back home.

I honestly didn't think I'd ever see him again.

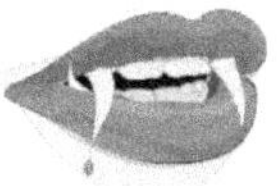

Home. My house did not fit my expectations when I opened the front door. I missed the endless forests of Faerie already, and the elegance of the elves' home. Even the Hunt's gray house had character compared to mine. I spent twenty minutes visualizing elaborate tapestries on my empty walls before I realized what I was doing and stopped.

I couldn't go to sleep. I couldn't concentrate on anything; every shifting shadow held a face; a new mystery. I had spent a day in Faerie, and lived to tell the tale. How could I continue my mundane existence?

But the human mind holds many a failsafe for coping with the shock of the supernatural. By the end of the next day, Sunday, I had fallen back into my normal groove again. I still jumped at shadows, but I couldn't quite remember why. Surrounded by my life, the reality of Faerie paled and shimmered like a half-forgotten dream or a mirage. In darkness, lying alone in bed, I could believe. In the cold light of reality, I could not.

I awoke Monday morning, my head filled with dreams I could not comprehend. The drive in to work took no time at all; my mind was not on the road. When I pulled into the parking lot, I saw Penny standing near the door, obviously waiting for me.

She pounced before I unbuckled my seat belt.

"Ms. Montgomery! You have to see this! I can't believe it!" She grabbed my arm and hauled me out of the car. I barely snatched my purse before the door slammed shut behind me. "I just wanted to get the mail from Saturday, and I...you have to see this!"

"Penny, are you feeling okay?" I lagged behind, even with her grip on my arm. "What happened?"

"I opened the mailbox and saw a strange package!"

A bomb! I thought. But who would want to bomb the library? "You didn't open it, did you?"

"Of course not. I can't even lift it. It weighs a ton. But one corner of the box was already open. The whole thing was covered in filth. It looked like it had been buried for *years.*"

Buried? Something awoke in the back of my mind. "Buried?" I asked weakly.

"You won't believe what's in the box," Penny said. "You won't *believe* it."

Out of the corner of my eye, I saw the director emerge from her cave. She sniffed the air, but I only smelled Penny's distinctive perfume. In the harsh fluorescent lights of the hallway, the director looked strange and unearthly, a rumpled heron, gangly and tall. I realized I had never seen her set foot in the hallway before. And how had she beat me to the office?

When she turned to stare at us, I noticed for the first time that her eyes were a deep shade of purple. She sniffed again.

At first, when Penny pulled me up to the mailbox, I didn't see the box. It lurked at the back in the shadows, smelling faintly of damp earth. I saw the torn corner, and a glint of what lay inside.

A glint. A *golden* glint.

With slightly shaking fingers, Penny held up a discolored gold coin. "As far as I can tell, that box is *full* of coins. Just like this one. Ms. Montgomery...do you think they're real?"

Full *of coins?*

Our director snatched the coin from Penny's fingers before I could speak. "This is Faerie gold." Penny and I stared at her. The director glowered. "Faerie gold."

Before we could react to this proclamation, the director reached into the mailbox, hefted the box into her arms, and walked back to her office, trailing gold coins as she went.

Penny stared after her, openmouthed. I picked up one of the fallen coins and stared down at it. I didn't recognize the profile or the writing or the country of origin. But the coin was whole and heavy in my hand, a testament to...a testament to a half-forgotten adventure. Had it only been one day?

"I couldn't even lift one end of the box," Penny whispered. "It...it left a dent in the bottom of the mailbox."

I couldn't think of a logical reply. My brain seemed to be frozen on the word *gold*.

"What's this?" Penny ducked into the mailbox and emerged with a folded piece of paper. She handed it to me. "It's addressed to you, Ms. Montgomery."

The thick paper rustled as I unfolded the note and read what was inside.

Bethany Dalton weighed one hundred and nine pounds.

The note was unsigned.

The director poked her head outside her door. "Karen? Can I see you in my office for a minute?" She spied the gold coins littering the carpet, and I swear her eyes began to glow. "Penny, will you pick those up?"

The battered cardboard box sat in the middle of the director's desk. One side had split entirely, and gold coins fought to spill from the crack. The director stood behind it, her expression a strange cross between confusion and greed.

"This box is addressed to you," she said.

"So was this note." I held it out to her, but she made no move to take it.

"Where were you all day Saturday? I tried to call you twice, but you didn't pick up."

"I...went on a short trip," I said, struggling with sticky disbelief.

"A short trip to where? You didn't pack for this trip, and you left right after you reset the alarm. Where did you go in the middle of the night?"

I had the insane urge to tell her everything, but I bit my tongue. True, she had claimed the gold to be Faerie gold, but how did she know?

The director sighed. "Karen, it will only help if you tell me." She took the note from my unresisting fingers, read it, and shook her head. "Ah. I see."

I cleared my throat. "You see what?"

"I'm tempted to bury this and forget it exists, but I'm sure you meant well," the director continued as if I hadn't spoken. I noticed she made no move to touch the gold. "Will this vanish in twenty-four hours? It smells real, but the elves are notorious for their trickery."

"It's supposed to be real," I whispered before I realized she said the 'e' word. "Wait a minute! You *knew* it was Faerie gold!"

"It stinks of magic," the director said. "I'm surprised you can't smell it."

I sank down in the chair in front of her desk. "I don't understand."

"Of course you don't. You weren't supposed to understand."

Her words made no sense. "What do you mean?"

The director ran one hand through her close-cropped hair and sighed. "Let me put it to you this way: Do you honestly believe Ivy Bedinghaus was the only supernatural being employed by the library system?"

I stared at her. "What? Who else?"

"Surely by now you must realize Beth-Hill isn't a normal Ohio town," the director said. "Even Amington isn't entirely mundane. The ratio of human and nonhuman residents are four times the norm, just in this county alone."

Sometimes, I'm a bit slow on the uptake. I remembered how she had lifted the heavy box of gold without breaking a sweat. How she never emerged from her...*cave* of an office during daylight hours, if she could help it.

"Is Penny human?" I *had* to know.

"Yes." The director smiled. Had her teeth grown longer or was it a trick of the light?

"Would it be rude to ask what you are?" I imagined it would be an irritating question; akin to a childless couple always having to answer why they had no offspring.

"Of course not." The director's smile widened.

I fought the sudden urge to back away. Her teeth *were* longer. "Are you an elf? A vampire?" *Another member of the Wild Hunt?*

"Goodness no!" The director leaned forward and rested her elbows on the box of gold. "*I* am a dragon."

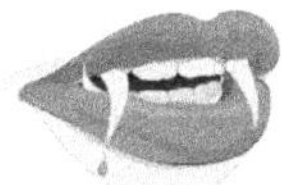

Three weeks later, I abandoned my office and the hounding of reporters to go on a little hike. The director had turned over all publicity about the library's miraculous bequeath to me, and I had been forced to hire an assistant to help me with my workload. It was a little tricky working around Ivy's limitations concerning the daylight hours, but we were managing to make it work.

I picked up the box of books on Penny's desk, a topographical map, and the invitations to the library's Christmas party were tucked safely inside my purse, and slipped out the door before anyone could stop me. I'd picked up some flyers on the way out as well, just in case the Master of the Wild Hunt was interested in storytime.

It took me nearly an hour to find the logging road I'd driven down in darkness, but I managed to find it. Lugging twenty pounds of books through heavy forest almost defeated my strength, but I remembered those earlier librarians who delivered their entire circulating collection by hand and persevered.

According to my map, the entire area was littered with caves, but the largest one--the Hunt's cave, or so I hoped--was a mere five-mile hike. At least I had worn better shoes this time around.

Three hours later, just as sunset cast long shadows across the forest, I found it again. I would have walked right past it if my arms hadn't given out; my map-reading skills were obviously lacking. But as I bent to retrieve my box, I heard a low growl behind me.

And a moment later, Nathaniel's voice. "I thought you gave your word never to come here again."

I turned to face him. He stood at the mouth of the cave with a Hound at his side. "Actually, you have my word that I wouldn't tell anyone where you lived."

His eyes kindled in the setting sun for a brief second before a rueful smile crossed his face. "You speak the truth. Why did you return? I heard you got your gold."

"The library got its gold," I said. "I wanted to thank you for your help."

He cocked an eyebrow. "You thanked me three weeks ago, but you return bearing...gifts?"

"Some of these are for Amalea," I said. "A complete set of Shakespeare, and some other poetry. I brought a handful of kids' books for..."

"The baby's name is Chloe," Nathaniel said, his face blank.

I smiled. "That's a beautiful name. These are the kinds of books that will last through puppy chewing, too. I asked."

"I'm...I'm not sure I want to know who you asked," Nathaniel said. "Did anyone follow you here?"

"No. And I didn't tell anyone where I was headed, either. Although...I think the director might suspect."

"Oh." He stood for a moment, lost in thought. "Would you...would you like to come in?" The Hound beside him stared up at him in shock. Nathaniel ignored it.

"I'd love to, but don't you have to ask permission first?" I had no desire to end up on the wrong foot with Gabriel.

Nathaniel's face cleared. "Ah. Yes." He ducked back into the cave, leaving the Hound on guard. A moment later, he returned. "You can come inside. Would you like me to carry your box?"

He lifted it with no apparent effort, and I discovered yet another thing to envy. Having Faerie blood did not give me miraculous strength or psychic powers, only an interesting footnote in my ancestry, and a marked reluctance to handle iron.

The Hound followed us inside, a baleful presence at my back.

Gabriel met us at the door. "You came back."

"She brought gifts," Nathaniel said, and lowered my box in front of the gray velvet couch. The Hound with the scars raised his head as I approached and gave me a curious glance. I smiled at him. The other Hound sniffed the box and glanced at his Master, as if silently berating Gabriel for letting me come in.

"Hush, Malachi," Gabriel murmured. "She means us no harm." He turned to me and waited, his eyes blank and cold.

"I wanted to thank Nathaniel again for his help," I said. "And since it's almost the holiday season..." My words fell into stiff silence, and I faltered to a stop.

"What did you bring?" When I glanced towards the scarred Hound, he was gone. In his place, a young man with the blue eyes of the Hound. His clothes covered the worst of the scars.

"Josiah..." Gabriel warned. The scarred Hound paid him no mind.

"Some books," I said, glad *someone* would speak to me. "A few things for the elves, if you have any way to reach them. A schedule for storytimes, if you think Chloe might like them." I dug in my purse. "And these."

The invitations were printed on Christmas cards, a snowy forest scene in which a flock of bright red cardinals decorated a tall pine tree. I had printed a dozen extra, since my scant knowledge of folklore had not told me how many Hounds made up the Wild Hunt. I gave one to Nathaniel, one to Gabriel, one to Josiah, and offered one to Malachi, but he ignored me.

Gabriel's brows drew down in a sharp vee as he read the invitation. "You want us to come to a *party?*"

A white haired woman appeared in the doorway on my left with Chloe in her arms. She smiled uncertainly when she saw me, so I gave her an invitation as well.

"I brought some books for Chloe, too," I told her.

She glanced at Gabriel. "Books?"

"She's a *librarian*," Gabriel said darkly. "What do you want in return?"

I realized, suddenly, why Nathaniel had been so surprised. The mere presence of gifts meant favors to be returned, exactly the same way Ivy had tricked him into bringing us both to Faerie.

"Nothing."

He glowered at me, disbelieving.

"Not a thing," I insisted. "I intended to ask Nathaniel if he would mind delivering a couple of invitations to Amalea and Kyren, but he doesn't *have* to do it."

Gabriel stared at his daughter, who had shifted into hound form to gnaw on the edge of the invitation. "I see. In exchange for your gifts you would have Nathaniel deliver invitations for you?"

Was the thought of a gift so alien to them? "No! I brought the books to thank Nathaniel and you, for helping me. The library will survive now. Ivy even got a new job."

"And if I refused to allow Nathaniel to deliver your invitations?" Gabriel asked.

I shrugged. "I'd find another way to get to Faerie and deliver them. But the books would stay here."

Josiah had crept up to the box while Gabriel's back was turned, and now sorted through some of the books. He held up a sheaf of white paper. "What are these?"

I had almost forgotten. "Library card applications."

Nathaniel shot me a startled look. "I thought...I thought you needed proof of your address to get a library card."

Gabriel's frown slowly melted away. He regarded his Hound silently, and I wondered if Nathaniel had told him about his secret trips to the library.

I smiled. "I don't think you have to worry about that anymore."

Nathaniel flushed under Gabriel's regard. And the Master of the Wild Hunt finally turned his gaze to me.

"Library cards are free," I said, trying to guess the question in his gaze. "You can check out as many books as you want from the library, and you have a certain amount of time to return them."

"And if you don't return them on time?" Josiah asked.

"Then you pay a fine."

Gabriel frowned again. "What kind of a fine?"

"It says ten cents per book, Gabriel." The white haired woman--Chloe's mother, I guessed--held out the pamphlet that came with the applications. "I don't think that's a lot of money."

"Emle..." Gabriel's voice dropped. He sighed. "Very well. Nathaniel, go find Eri and Brenna and bring them here. How many of you want library cards?"

Even then, I half-expected the Wild Hunt to skip the Christmas party. But they arrived in style with Amalea, Kyren, and a handful of elves who treated our guests to a rousing ceilidh in the middle of the library, and the rafters have not been the same ever since.

The End

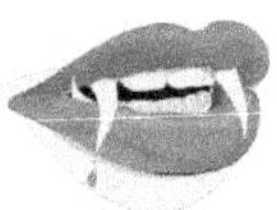

You can find ALL our books up at r on our website at:

http://www.writers-exchange.com

All Jennifer's books:

http://www.writers-exchange.com/Jennifer-St-Clair/

all our fantasy novels:

http://www.writers-exchange.com/category/genres/fantasy/

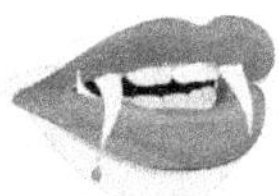

About the Author

Jennifer St. Clair grew up in Southern Ohio and spent most of her childhood in the woods around her home. She wrote her first novel when she was thirteen, and hasn't stopped since. She lives with her ball python, Fester, and two cats, Ash and Rowan.

In her spare time, she crochets, makes cloth dolls, collects antiques, books, and vintage clothing, and takes digital photographs with varying degrees of success.

Her *Beth-Hill series* is set in the area in America that contains many supernatural creatures: Wild Hunt, Vampires, Dragons, Faery and more.

It is part of the Universe that her *Jacob Lane Series*, *Karen Montgomery Series* and vampire trilogy, *The Shadow Series* are set in.

Follow all her books on her author page:
http://www.writers-exchange.com/Jennifer-St-Clair/

If you want to read more about other books by this author, they are listed on the following pages...

A Beth-Hill Novel (Stand Alone Novels)

Are creatures of the night and all manner of extramundane beings drawn to certain locations in the natural world? In the Midwestern village of Beth-Hill located in southern Ohio, the population is made up of its fair share of common citizens...and much more than its share of supernatural residents. Take a walk on the wild side in this unusual place where imagination meets reality.

Blood of Innocents

Ten years ago, Orien, crown prince of the Seleighe, was captured by his mortal enemies, locked in a dungeon and turned into a vampire. Six years into Orien's sentence, the Healer's brother Cullen disobeyed his mistress's orders to kill him and turned him into a vampire instead, thus sealing both their fates for all eternity.

Now both Orien and Cullen are set free. But a secret only Cullen knows lies locked inside his mind, threatening to drive him mad before he can uncover the identity of a traitor--the very elf who betrayed Orien and left them both to die in darkness.

Publisher: http://www.writers-exchange.com/blood-of-innocents/

Full Moon

Werewolves change into wolves when the moon is full. But Edward's curse only allows him to be *human* when the moon is full.

Alone and despairing, Edward hides himself away from the world. He's scraped out a meager existence for himself for almost a century in the forest he's grown to love and call home. But in the depths of a terrible winter, he stumbles across clues from the life his mother left behind in Faerie. The truth may give him the answers he needs about the source of his birthright... and the curse that holds him captive.

Publisher: http://www.writers-exchange.com/full-moon/

A Beth-Hill Novel: Jacob Lane Series

Are creatures of the night and all manner of extramundane beings drawn to certain locations in the natural world? In the Midwestern village of Beth-Hill located in southern Ohio, the population is made up of its fair share of common citizens...and much more than its share of supernatural residents.

Jacob Lane is a ten-year-old girl who's spent her life unaware of her magical heritage. After being sent to Darkbrook, a school of magic, supernatural mysteries seem to spring to life all around her and her new friends.

Book 1: The Tenth Ghost

After Jacob Lane's parents mysteriously vanish, she's sent to Darkbrook, the only school of magic in the United States. While there, she and her new friends stumble upon a series of mysterious deaths in the nine ghosts that haunt the halls of Darkbrook. These ghosts were students who died at the school over the past hundred years. Will Jacob become the tenth ghost, or can she stop a witch's reign of terror?

Publisher: http://www.writers-exchange.com/the-tenth-ghost/

Book 2: The Ninth Guest

When Jacob's friend Ophelia's family decides to open up their castle for guests, amateur paranormal sleuth Jacob Lane is invited to join in on the fun. "Spend the night in a vampire's castle and live to tell the tale!" is supposed to be a fundraiser to help Ophelia's family pay the bills. Heating a castle costs quite a bit, after all. But, after the truth of an old secret is uncovered, what began as an innocent business venture soon turns deadly when vampire hunters get involved.

For years, the vampire hunters have had only one goal: To destroy all vampires. With the help of a new friend, Jacob and Ophelia must work together to save the entire VonBriggle family from extinction.

Publisher: http://www.writers-exchange.com/the-ninth-guest/

Book 3: The Eighth Room

For two hundred years, the Selkies have kept themselves separate from those who live on land. But now the Selkies need allies or they'll be crushed by their ancient enemies, the Finfolk.

Jacob and Ophelia, students at the only school of magic in the United States, uncover a mystery that dates back to Darkbrook's beginnings. While helping clean out old storage rooms for classroom expansion, they find something that might save the Selkies from extinction. With the help of the youngest member of the Wild Hunt who are no longer so wild or terrifying, they must foil the Finfolk who desire the Selkie's destruction...or die trying.

Publisher: http://www.writers-exchange.com/the-eighth-room/

Book 4: The Seventh Secret

After a picture of Niklas, the dragons' liaison to the only school of magic in the United States, shows up in too many newspapers to count, Darkbrook is forced to go on the defensive. The secret of Darkbrook's existence has been discovered. But there are more than dragonhunters in the forest, and, as Jacob Lane, supernatural sleuth and student at Darkbrook, learns how to use her newly discovered talent of healing, she helps to right an old wrong and must battle a teenaged wizard intent on proving--once and for all--that magic is real.

Publisher: http://www.writers-exchange.com/the-seventh-secret/

Book 5: The Sixth Stone

Jacob Lane, supernatural sleuth, and Danny, her werewolf friend, stumble across an alternate world where the Wild Hunt was never bound, and Darkbrook, the school of magic they attend, was abandoned a hundred years ago.

But when the Hounds of the Hunt wish to surrender, the two students are swept up in a whirlwind of heartbreak, betrayal, and the discovery of a lost treasure.

Publisher: http://www.writers-exchange.com/the-sixth-stone/

A Beth-Hill Novella: Karen Montgomery Series

Are creatures of the night and all manner of extramundane beings drawn to certain locations in the natural world? In the Midwestern village of Beth-Hill located in southern Ohio, the population is made up of its fair share of common citizens...and much more than its share of supernatural residents. Take a walk on the wild side in this unusual place where imagination meets reality.

Karen Montgomery was an ordinary woman until she stumbled into the extraordinary... A bargain with elves worth its weight in gold. A plague of sinister ladybugs. Rogue vampire hunters, including one who tries to turn over a new leaf--with disastrous consequences. A ghostly huntsmen of the Wild Hunt wishing for redemption. Karen's life will never be the same again.

Book 1: Budget Cuts

Karen Montgomery is used to taking care of the unpleasant jobs no one else wants to deal with. When a shortage of funds forces her to fire fifteen employees from the library, she isn't happy, but the nasty task has to be done and she is, after all, the boss. But Karen finds finishing her task impossible when she can't seem to track down Ivy Bedinghaus, a night clerk she's never actually met. Once she finally does confront Ivy, she's thrust into a centuries-old conflict that makes her previous troubles radically pale in comparison.

Publisher: http://www.writers-exchange.com/budget-cuts/

Book 2: The Secret of Redemption

Karen Montgomery, librarian, finds herself embroiled in another otherworldly adventure...

A member of the Wild Hunt--ghostly myths that aren't so ghostly (or myth-like) anymore--needs help in reconciling who he once was in life and who he is now.

A little girl has gone missing. And the one most likely responsible for her disappearance is the one Karen must prove innocent.

Publisher: http://www.writers-exchange.com/the-secret-of-redemption/

Book 3: Ladybug, Ladybug

An innocent attempt to rid the library of a plague of ladybugs turns sinister when a rogue vampire hunter gets the contract for pest control.

Ivy Bedinghaus, who works for Karen as a night clerk--along with all the vampires in Beth-Hill--are in danger, and their only hope for survival is with the help of Karen, a member of the Wild Hunt, and Russell Moore, a reformed vampire hunter.

Publisher: http://www.writers-exchange.com/ladybug-ladybug/

Book 4: Detour

One wrong turn sends Karen down a road that shouldn't exist, to the site of an old accident and an even older mystery. With reformed vampire hunter Russell Moore's help, Karen finds the key to the mystery. But Russ keeps his own secrets...some of which are deadly.

When old friends from Russ' past come to call, Karen realizes his secrets might just mean his doom. After a terrible incident three years ago, before Karen met him, Russ wants only to live the rest of his life quietly in Beth-Hill. But his secret might not allow him the new lease on life Russ longs for.

Publisher: http://www.writers-exchange.com/detour/

Companion Story: Russ' Story: Capture

Long before Russell Moore ever met supernatural sleuth Karen Montgomery or set foot in Beth-Hill, he was a vampire hunter, possibly the best vampire hunter of all. He brought down whole nests of vampires, caring little about the consequences of his actions. Anyone who lived with or helped the vampires became enemies to be slaughtered.

So what kind of an idiot would capture a ruthless vampire hunter without a conscience and try to reform him?

Ethan Walker was that idiot. Wanting to protect his family, Ethan set out to prove to Russ that vampires weren't all evil, soulless creatures. If Russ would allow himself to witness their lives, see their humanity, surely he and other vampire hunters like him would let them live in peace. *Surely?*

Publisher: http://www.writers-exchange.com/capture/

Secrets When in Shadow Lie

Twelve years ago, Ryan Grey was cursed by a witch to hide a secret. He's lived with the curse of being unable to die permanently, and, over the years he's slowly losing the memory of his past until almost nothing remains.

But now, after a chance meeting with an elf named Zipporah, he discovers the key to unlocking the secret and breaking the curse once and for all...if he can survive the breaking.

Publisher: http://www.writers-exchange.com/secrets-when-in-shadow-lie/

The Dead Who Do Not Sleep

Will Spark only wants a good night's sleep after a night of drinking. Instead, two thugs bang on his door, demanding answers to questions he can't understand. And then they killed him...

Publisher: http://www.writers-exchange.com/the-dead-who-do-not-sleep/

A Beth-Hill Novel: The Abby Duncan Series

Are creatures of the night and all manner of extramundane beings drawn to certain locations in the natural world? In the Midwestern village of Beth-Hill located in southern Ohio, the population is made up of its fair share of common citizens...and much more than its share of supernatural residents. Take a walk on the wild side in this unusual place where imagination meets reality.

Situated in Beth-Hill, where imagination meets reality, is The Rose Emporium, owned by elderly and not-a-little-odd Rose Duncan. The large Victorian house smackdab in the middle of nowhere is a cross between a pawn shop and an antique store that caters to supernatural creatures needing to barter. Rose's twenty-something niece, Abby Duncan, discovers that the world isn't made up of just run-of-the-mill, ordinary humans but an entire spectrum of unusual beings. With her preconceptions about what's normal and what's not turned upside-down, Abby is in for a whole lot of startling truths, mysteries-- about herself and the people and places around her--and danger.

Novella 1: By Any Other Name

Woodturner Abby Duncan decides to sell her spindles at a local Renaissance Festival with only some success. After all, no one really spins their own yarn anymore, do they? While there, she discovers that one of her newfound friends is not what he appears--and his secret is about to get him killed!

Publisher: http://www.writers-exchange.com/by-any-other-name/

Book 2: The Uncrowned Queen

Abby Duncan's elderly Aunt Rose has always been a bit odd. And now she's off on a mysterious trip, leaving Abby behind to run the Rose Emporium, an unusual sort of antique shop. Such an extraordinary store would have been a perfect place for Seth and the others, her friends from the Renaissance Festival, to take a break from traveling between Faires. But when tragedy strikes and Abby and the others discover the true nature of the Rose Emporium, they'll have to travel into Faerie itself before their tightknit group is whole again.

Abby doesn't know much about her family history, but she's about to find out the truth...whether she likes it or not.

Publisher: http://www.writers-exchange.com/the-uncrowned-queen/

Book 3: Coming Soon!

A Beth-Hill Novel: The Shadows Trilogy

Are creatures of the night and all manner of extramundane beings drawn to certain locations in the natural world? In the Midwestern village of Beth-Hill located in southern Ohio, the population is made up of its fair share of common citizens...and much more than its share of supernatural residents. Take a walk on the wild side in this unusual place where imagination meets reality.

A Dreamer dreams the future when the past is not yet laid to rest. Ten years ago, a plague swept across the Seven Kingdoms. Ten years ago, the Queen of Iomar's son was exiled and named the author of the magical plague. Now, in the present, Terrin works to complete his ultimate goal: Control of the Seven Kingdoms using his son's power to supplement his own. But his attempt at dominion meets resistance and the fate of the world rests in the unlikely hands of an exiled prince, a Dreamer, and a vampire...

Book 1: The Prince of Shadows

When Alban's father Terrin appeared at the castle door with a vampire in tow and apologies on his lips, Alban fell under his spell just like everyone else and welcomed him home. But Terrin didn't return to live quietly in his brother's kingdom. He had other plans and, with Alban's untrained powers at his disposal, he begins his ruthless plan to destroy the Seven Kingdoms and rule them all, beginning with his brother's death.

Terrin engineers events to cast the blame on his nephew, Teluride, intending to see the boy executed for his father's murder. But there are those who would thwart Terrin in his mad plan for power, and Alban forms an unlikely alliance with Skade, the reclusive Queen of Iomar, and Terrin's slave, a young vampire with no memory of his name or origins. Although the future looks grim, Alban and the vampire attempt to stop Terrin...and they almost succeed.

A darker history lies at the heart of Terrin's treachery, and only Skade knows the true reason why Terrin would murder his own brother and attempt to destroy both Alban and the vampire to achieve his goals. The Ghost who resides in Skade's mirror--her servant and thrall--holds one of the keys to Terrin's madness. Unfortunately, more than one person wishes for the past to remain the past and the future to hold no shadows of what might have been...

Publisher: http://www.writers-exchange.com/the-prince-of-shadows/

Book 2: Lost In Shadows

Events set in motion ten years ago come to a head as Skade, the reclusive Queen of Iomar, and Nicodemus, who is imprisoned by Skade, struggle to free Alban and the vampire from Terrin's grasp. Old secrets come to light when Skade's exiled son is forced to face his past--or die trying to redeem himself once and for all. Can the crimes of the past truly be forgiven? Only time will tell...and time is running out.

Publisher: http://www.writers-exchange.com/lost-in-shadows/

Book 3: Bound In Shadows

With his power crushed, brother to the king and father to Alban, Terrin is forced to take drastic measures to regain his sons after they are freed and harness the power they possess. But he has an ally inside the healer's house where they are recovering who works to further his plans. The Queen of Iomar, Skade's son, courts redemption to try to save his mother's life, and the vampire who no longer remembers his own name dreams a dream that might save them all...or damn them if success is thwarted.

Publisher: http://www.writers-exchange.com/bound-in-shadows/

A Beth-Hill Novel: Wild Hunt Series

Are creatures of the night and all manner of extramundane beings drawn to certain locations in the natural world? In the Midwestern village of Beth-Hill located in southern Ohio, the population is made up of its fair share of common citizens...and much more than its share of supernatural residents. Take a walk on the wild side in this unusual place where imagination meets reality.

The Wild Hunt roamed the forest outside of Beth-Hill until the Council bound them for a hundred years. Nevertheless, a century of existence has made an indelible mark not easily forgotten for these ghostly myths that are no longer so ghostly or myth-like...

Book 1: Heart's Desire

The Wild Hunt roamed the forest outside of Beth-Hill until the Council bound them for a hundred years--a lifetime for a human but only a passing thought to one such as Gabriel, Master of the Wild Hunt. As the Council's binding draws to a close, old enemies reappear to ensure that the Wild Hunt is bound once more--to a creature much worse than the Council has been.

Publisher: http://www.writers-exchange.com/hearts-desire/

Book 2: Fire and Water

As a young vampire, Erialas Morgan brought his mother back to life with a spell that shouldn't exist, shouldn't have worked...perhaps shouldn't have been performed at all. Desperation and love are his only excuses for doing the unthinkable.

There are others who wish to use that same spell for their own gain--and to destroy the Wild Hunt once and for all. Caught in the middle of a war between the Morgan clan of vampires and their human kin, Erialas turns to the Hunt for help. But even Gabriel, the Master of the Wild Hunt, may not be able to stop the tide of death and destruction once it turns.

Publisher: http://www.writers-exchange.com/fire-and-water/

Book 3: The Lost

Almost sixty years ago, Darkbrook, the only school of magic in the United States, opened its doors to students of decidedly different natures, sending out letters of invitation to the elves, the dragons, and the vampires. The three who responded to the invitation banded together despite their differences but vanished only weeks later along with an entire classroom full of students and their teacher after a field trip gone horribly wrong.

The Wild Hunt has healed and the Hounds have grown closer together, keeping Darkbrook's forest safe and secure for those who live there. Malachi, one of the eldest members of the Wild Hunt, has adapted to Josiah's spell to help him see, but when a demon boy trapped in the body of a human body for sixty years inside the school disrupts the newfound calm, the Hunt--and those they protect--are thrust into a struggle that should have ended long ago when a vampire, an elf, and a dragon vanished into the Mists.

Publisher: http://www.writers-exchange.com/the-lost/

Book 4: A Glint of Silver

Jericho is a vampire who wants is to live away from the Richmond household of vampires led by his ruthless father Connor. When Jericho tries to escape, Connor punishes him and leaves him to die. Tristan is determined to be the one to bring Jericho back, but he can't see him suffer for wanting a normal life. As long as Connor lives, Jericho will never be safe or free. As long as Connor *lives*...

Publisher: http://www.writers-exchange.com/a-glint-of-silver/

Book 5: All That Glitters

As a member of the cruel Morgan Household of vampires, twelve-year-old Arthur Morgan has been abused all his life.

Maya, a water fairy, shows him just how horrible and twisted the household he's grown up is. With her help, and the unexpected help of an adult vampire, Arthur attempts to escape.

Can he become something more than what his father has decreed?

Publisher: http://www.writers-exchange.com/all-that-glitters/

The Chelsea Chronicles

Normally a quiet, serene place, Chelsea Kingdom seems like the perfect location for a centuries' old vampire to blend in and live a normal life, even escape hunters and an angry mob. Unfortunately, his timing couldn't be worse...

Book 1: So You Want to be a Vampire

Chelsea Kingdom is usually a pretty quiet place but recent murders--committed by a vampire--upset the calm. Newcomer to town, Vlad Dhalgren wants only to blend in and live a normal life. He quickly learns that isn't possible, given that other vampires have been hiding in the shadows around the castle--in plain sight--for years.

Despite her lineage, Anna Everett, the crown princess of the Kingdom of Chelsea, isn't a wizard like her father, which means she will never be Queen. She has only one friend, Valerian Moreton--Val--who has secrets he's never shared that could get him *and* Anna killed...

Publisher: http://www.writers-exchange.com/so-you-want-to-be-a-vampire/

Book 2: Transformation

As Anna, crown princess of Chelsea, adjusts to life as a vampire after recent events, Vlad plans for a future he has no real hope to seeing come to pass due to injuries sustained while attempting to save Anna's life. But, as life goes on for Anna and her friend Valerian "Val" Moreton, it changes for others--some of whom are not quite what they seem...

Publisher: http://www.writers-exchange.com/transformation/

www.ingramcontent.com/pod-product-compliance
Lightning Source LLC
Chambersburg PA
CBHW052221150726
48002CB00003B/1213